FROM THE AUTHOR

Hello my lovely readers,

Soaked In My tears is a new book, but it has characters that are from the Anthology A Fistful Of Love Volume 2. I just wanted to let you guys know in case some of the character names sound familiar. No you don't have to read the Anthology story first. You can if you like, but it's not necessary. Thanks again for rocking with me. I hope you enjoy........

SUBSCRIBE

Text Shan to 22828 to stay up to date with new releases, sneak peeks, contest, and more...

Or sign up Here

Check your spam if you don't receive an email thanking you for signing up.

Interested in being apart of Shan Presents? Send submission to submissions@shanpresents.com

DEJA

Tiombe kept getting on my nerves for me to go out with her today, but I wasn't beat. I knew I needed a night out since I've been locked up in the house for the past couple of weeks.

"Bitch, why are you sitting in the back seat like you lost your best friend."

"I'm good, just got some shit on my mind, that's all."

"Well we ready to hit club Lacura, so that you can twerk something." I just looked at her crazy ass and started laughing. She always wanted to party.

"You crazy as hell, girl."

"I know, that's why you love me. Where's Jace crazy ass at? We don't need him coming up in here acting a damn fool like he always does."

"He's been out of town for a couple of days on business, and he is not coming back until tomorrow night," Tiombe looked at me with the side eye.

"What business that nigga handling?"

"Come on Tee, don't start."

I didn't feel like hearing her talking down about my man. That was one thing I hated about her.

My name is Deja Simmons, Tiombe Shields and I had been BFF's since we were born. We both were born in raised in Atlanta, Georgia. Our mothers were best friends, just like us. At the age of twenty-three, we both were attending Clark-Atlanta University. Even though I had taken a semester off due to personal reasons, I was gone make sure to sign up for the next semester.

"I'm gone let you live tonight, but you gone here it all tomorrow."

Tiombe couldn't stand Jace they never got along, and they did nothing but argue. Most of the time, I just stayed away from her to keep the peace between the two. I was shocked that Tiombe still fucked with me since I would push her to the side often.

We were now pulling up to the club, and the line was down the damn street. I hated this place, but I knew I could use a drink or two. Tee grabbed my arm and pulled me to the front of the line.

"Come on, my boo thing is the bouncer tonight."

I didn't know who she was talking about because she had many friends. Once we made it in, we walked straight to the bar.

"Hey Reesy, let me get two double shots of Crown Royal Vanilla." I said to the barmaid.

"You got it, beautiful," Reesy's ass always was flirting with me. I had to tell her that I didn't do girls a couple of times. I was so oblivious when she first came onto me, not even knowing she wanted me. She handed us our shots and I gave her the cash.

"Keep them coming too, Reesy," I said while I threw my shot back. Then, all of a sudden *Rake it up by. Yo Gotti ft. Nikki Minaj* was blaring through the speakers and the crowd went crazy.

I tell all my hoes, rake up
Break it down, back up
Fuck it up, fuck it up, back it up, back it up
Rake it up, rake it up, back it up, back it up

Tee and I ran to the dance floor and did exactly what the song said. We were definitely fucking it up. I was all in a zone, getting it, until I felt my arm being pulled out of socket. I was yanked so hard I felt that shit.

"What the fuck you doing here, Deja?" Jace barked.

"OUCH, JACE! Get off me, don't do this in here."

I guess Tee finally realized I wasn't dancing with her anymore. Once she saw Jace dragging me by my arm out the door she ran behind us.

"Jace, get the fuck off of her. You are always showing ya ass out here."

"Tee mind ya fucking business. What goes on between my girl and me ain't got shit to do with you."

"Nigga, fuck you. It has everything to do with me," Tee said while trying to jump on his back. Jace grabbed her and threw her on the ground. I went to help her up off the ground.

"Deja, go get the fuck in the car, now."

I looked at him and Tee. The look in Jace eye's told me that if I didn't take my ass to the car, he was gone fuck me up. Then I looked at Tee and she shook her head and got up, then headed back into the club. I knew I fucked up and my friend probably wasn't gone fuck with me ever again. Once I made it to the car, the doors were already unlocked, so I got in the passenger seat. About five minutes later, Jace was hopping in the car.

"What the fuck are you doing outside, Deja? You should be home. You ain't got no business being in no club with ya hoe ass friend, shaking ya ass."

Me not responding angered him, but I didn't give a fuck. He grabbed a hand full of my curly hair and turned my head, so I was now facing him.

"That hurts, Jace."

"I know it hurts, but I can see ya ass can talk, so answer me. What the fuck was you doing outside?"

"I needed to get out. I've been locked up in the house for weeks, Jace. It's fucking boring. You don't even stay home anymore. You made me stop going to school to be home with you and you're never there. How you expect me to stay in the house and you're never there."

"I don't give a damn about all of that. Keep ya ass in the house until I say you can go out. As for you hanging with Tee, dead that shit or I'll kill both y'all asses. Do you understand me?"

I nodded my head and he kissed my cheek then let my hair go. I leaned my head on the window and cried silent tears. Jace McCray and I have been together since I was eighteen and he was twenty. When we met, I just knew I found the love of my life until the abuse started. My mom loves her some Jace, only because she doesn't know that he's been beating my ass for the past couple of years. Tee doesn't know, either. She might see him grip me up and shit like that, but she hasn't seen the bruises and black eyes. I stay away from her when I'm really fucked up, but I still talk to her on the phone. She just thinks Jace is a jealous boyfriend, and her not liking him keeps her away from my home.

I'm starting to get tired of this situation. He doesn't even want me out of the house. I have no job. I'm not even in school right now. He feels like he makes enough money out on these streets to take care of me, so why do I need to be outside. The car was quiet all the way home. The good part about that was he already said what he had to say, so he was done with being angry. When we made it home it would be like nothing ever happened.

JACE

I was packing my bag about to go home when I got a phone call that Deja was at Club Lacura. My blood was boiling because nobody told her ass to go outside.

"You good, baby?" Miko asked while I was packing my bag.

"Yes I'm good baby, just need to go handle some business."

"Alright, when will you be back."

"I'll be back later on in the week."

Amiko was some chick I've been dealing with for about a year. She knows all about Deja and my street life, and it doesn't bother her. As long as I spend time with her when she wants, she's fine with whatever I do. Miko has been married before, and she's older than me. After her divorce she said the relationship thing wasn't for her. She would rather stay single and do her, because she doesn't have time for these cheating ass niggas. Shit, that was music to my ears. I was able to do me, so I didn't give a fuck.

After I packed my shit, I kissed Miko on her lips and headed out the door. My first stop was the club. I made it there in about ten minutes. I was still in town. I had Deja thinking I was away on business. As I was pulling up, I noticed it was a crowd in the club parking lot, which told me I was gone be in and out. My boy Big Will was the one that called and told me about Deja being at the club. He knows I didn't play about my girl, Deja just didn't know how many people I had keeping an eye on her sneaky little ass.

When I entered the club I saw Tee's hoe ass and Deja twerking. I walked up to her and snatched her ass right up, she didn't even know it was me. After I dragged her little ass out of the club, of course I knew her little BFF, or whatever the fuck she calls her, was gone to jump bad. I didn't feel like this shit tonight at all. Once she jumped on my back, I flung her little ass on the ground and made Deja go to the car. Then I followed behind her. After that, all I wanted to do was go home. I was tired and just wanted to lay up under Deja. I wasn't gone beat her ass tonight. We had a little conversation while sitting in the car and she agreed to everything I said. I was cool with that so we could go home and chill. A half hour had past and we were now pulling up to our home. I tapped Deja on the leg to wake her up.

"Come baby, we home."

She didn't say anything, she just opened the door and hopped out. I knew she was in her feelings, but I didn't care. She would be over it in the morning. I hopped out of the car and locked it up, then entered my house. It was nice and clean in here, like always. Deja even had dinner in the microwave for me. This girl was my life. I know it might seem like I don't love her, but I really do. Deja is my everything and she is never leaving me. She would die first before she ever leaves this relationship, and I meant that shit.

"Do you want me to heat your food up for you?"

"Nah, I got it. Just go ahead and shower, and go to bed. I'll be up there after I eat."

Deja did what I told her while I heated my food up. I heard my phone going off alerting me that I had a text message. When I looked at the phone I saw I had a picture text from Miko. When I saw a picture of a positive pregnancy test, I almost lost it. She knew damn well I didn't want any damn kids by anybody but Deja.

Me: *And what were you gone do about it.*

Miko: *I don't know Jace I'm almost thirty and I want kids.*

Me: *you already know what it is Ma.*

Miko: *I'll raise it by myself Jace I just thought I'd let you know.*

I didn't say shit else, I just turned my phone off, grabbed my plate, and started eating. This shit was crazy. I knew what Miko said was true. I knew she would handle her business I just didn't need this shit to come back and bite me in the ass. While eating my food, I was in deep thought. I didn't hear any noise upstairs so Deja was probably now in the bed.

After I finished my food, I washed my plate and headed for my shower. Once I walked in my room, Deja was sprawled out on the bed, knocked out. I could see that she was ass naked through the thin sheet she had covering her body. Baby girl was so beautiful, all of a sudden, I started feeling like shit because of the way I treated her. I needed to get my shit together, she didn't deserve any of what I was doing to her.

After staring at her for a couple of seconds, I stripped out of my clothes, walked to my bathroom, and turned the water onto the temperature I liked, then hopped in. I washed and rinsed a couple of times, then shut the water off and hopped out. Once I dried off and wrapped the towel around my waist, I headed to my room, took the towel off, and climbed into the bed. I pulled Deja close to me and kissed her forehead. She stared up and looked at me with a little attitude because I woke her.

"I'm sorry baby, I had to move you over," I whispered and she closed her eyes. I wrapped my arms around her and drifted off to sleep.

* * *

The sun shining in my window woke me up out of my sleep. A nigga was still tired, it felt like I had just taken my ass to sleep. I looked on the side of me, and Deja was still sleeping. I figured since it's been a minute since we've been out I would take her out to breakfast and to do a little shopping. I pulled her close to me, then kissed her forehead, the tip of her nose, and her lips.

"Wake up, beautiful." Her eyes opened and she was staring at me.

"Good morning Jace," she said, just above a whisper.

"You wanna spend the day with your man," I asked.

"Sure, why not. I ain't doing shit around here." I knew she was being sarcastic, but I was gone let it slide. I knew she was still upset about last night.

"Come on baby, don't be like that. I'm sorry about last night."

"I know you're sorry, Jace. Now let me sleep for another hour or two."

"Ok, you got that, but can you show your man how much you miss him before you go back to sleep?"

She looked at me and smiled as she slid under the covers. As soon as I felt her warm breath on my dick, my shit bricked right up. She licked the head of it, and then swallowed my shit whole. No matter how bad shit got between Deja and me, sex was always the shit. After she sucked on my mans for a little, she came from under the covers and climbed on top of me. It took her a little bit to adjust to my size. Then, once she was the way she wanted to be, she rode the shit out of my dick just the way I liked it.

"Damn girl, go ahead and show me how much you miss me," I cooed while my toes were curling.

Deja's ass then turned around quick as hell and started riding me reverse cowgirl style. I hated when she did this shit, because watching her ass bounce up and down did something to me and made me bust fast as hell.

"FUCK MA!" I said while I was shooting my seeds right up in her ass.

I wanted kids with Deja, but I knew our relationship wasn't healthy. So, I didn't mind her taking birth control. I needed my life in order before I could be someone's daddy. That's why I was pissed off about Miko's ass being pregnant. I know I should be using protection with her ass, but shit be happening in the heat of the moment.

"You good, Jace?" Deja asked while kissing my lips bringing me out of my thoughts.

"Shit baby, after that shit you just put on me, I'm more than good. A nigga is great."

Deja laughed at me then laid her head on my chest. I pushed the thought about Miko being pregnant to the back of my head, and closed my eyes so I could take this nap with Deja before we got our day started.

TAJI

I was at the airport waiting for my cousin Tyreem to pick me up. My dad and I thought it would be a good idea to spend some time with him in ATL. By the way, my name is Taji Price, and I'm twenty-three years old. See I was a different type from all the men in my family. They all were in the street life, except for me. My dad wanted me to take over his business, but I didn't want to. I'm into music, so I was thinking about opening up a couple of studios, or even being a producer. I also could sing my ass off, so I wanted to do a little of everything in the music business.

My dad got mad money, but me being in the music life wasn't his plans for me. So, if this is what I wanted to do, I had to get it on my own. Tyreem respected what I wanted to do, so he said he would help me get started. We didn't tell my dad what was going on, he thinks I'm down here just visiting Reem for a little while to get away from Camden. When I told him that he said, 'go ahead maybe you need a vacation to get your mind right'. He also told me to be ready to take over when I get back. I brushed that shit off and went on with my plan. My phone started ringing. I looked to see who it was, and Reem's name flashed across my screen.

"Yo, cuz come on. I'm out front."

"Ok, here I come now."

I hurried and grabbed my bags and ran out the airport. Reem and I hadn't seen each other in years. Once I made it to the car, he hopped out and pulled me in for a one arm hug.

"Hey, look at you looking all grown in shit," Reem said while laughing.

"Nigga, shut up. I am grown." We both hopped in the car.

"Ok, you got two choices. You could stay in my crib with my girl and me. It's big as hell, so you'll have your own space. Or you can stay at a hotel. It's your choice."

"I don't mind staying with you, cuz."

"Alright, well let's go then." Reem headed to his home. I'd never met his girl, but I'd heard nothing but great things about her.

"So, how're things going down here for you. Do you ever wanna move back home?"

"Nah, this is originally where I'm from, so once I came back to my hometown, I never had any intentions of going back to Jersey."

" I feel like Jersey is not for me anymore, especially for what I wanna do."

"Well you a grown ass man, cuz. Do what makes you happy. Ya daddy might not like it, but he'll get over it. Just do your thing and make him happy."

"Thanks Reem, I really appreciate all your words of encouragement. You don't know how much all those late night conversations help me after many arguments with his ass. I swear my dad is a stubborn man. It's either his way or no way." Reem burst out laughing.

"I know exactly what you mean. Shit, I use to live with y'all. Your dad didn't talk to me for months when I moved back down here." We were now pulling up to Reem's big ass home. The beautiful chick, who I assumed was his girl, was sitting on the step, while two little boys who looked like they were twins ran around the yard. As soon as Reem parked and got out the car, both the boys ran his way screaming "daddy". I grabbed my things out of the car and followed Reem up to the steps.

"Hey baby, how are you doing?" Reem asked.

"I'm good, just brought the boys out here for some fresh air. Hello Taji, how are you? I'm Bailey," she said while she held her hand out to shake mine.

"Hello Bailey, nice to meet you, and thanks for allowing me to stay in your home."

"Awwwww, no thanks needed. Any family of Reem's is welcome anytime. Reem will show you where your room is, and let me know if you need anything. Dinner will be ready in an hour."

"Come on cuz, let's go," Reem said, showing me to my room.

"Damn cuz, this house big as shit. You doing big things down here, I see."

"Thanks, and this is where you will be staying. You have your own bathroom. The company is cool, just let me know ahead of time and who they are. Of course, you don't have a curfew, but let me know when you are not coming home."

"Alright cuz, I got you." Once I put all my shit away,y my phone alerted me that I had a text message.

Monae: *Did you make it there safe.*

Me: *Yes, I'm good Ma.*

Monae: *Imma miss you so much Taj.*

Me: *I haven't even been gone a whole day Monae.*

Monae: *I know Taj, but I that you're not here.*

I didn't even respond to her last text. Her ass was so full of shit. Monae was this chick that I fucked from time to time. I was feeling her until I found out she only was fucking with me because of who I was. Once I found out her ass was a fraud, I just stopped spending time with her and fucked her when I wanted to.

See, bitches where I was from would let me do whatever the fuck I wanted to just because of who I was. That shit got old to me. I wanted a queen. Somebody that I can give the world, somebody that loved me for who I was, not because of what my last name was. The Price family rang bells in Jersey. Everywhere I went they knew who I was and that shit was annoying. I feel like I'm gone enjoy my stay here in Atlanta. I looked at my phone, seeing that it was now time for dinner, so I headed downstairs to eat. That hour went by so damn fast. When

I made it to the dining room, Reem was sitting at the table, and the twins were in their high chairs making all types of noises.

"How old are they cuz, and what's there names?"

"They are three and their names are Braylon and Braxton."

"They look like they are a handful."

"These little niggas run this house. They keep us busy." I looked at him and started laughing.

"Shit, they don't run nothing but Reem, he let them do whatever they want," Bailey said while bringing the twins their food. After she sat their food in front of them she went to get me and Reem's plates.

"Don't start Bailey, I do not let them do whatever they want," Reem got so defensive. I had a feeling she was telling the truth from the look on his face. Once Bailey gave everyone their food we all sat, ate, and talked.

"So, what's on the agenda for the night? Reem are you taking Taj out for the night to see how we do in the A."

"Yeah, I figured he could hang out with us tonight. I don't know where we are going, but Bro said he was down." I didn't know they had plans on taking me out, but I was all for it.

"Oh Lawd, you got my brother to come out tonight." I remember hearing about Bro, but I didn't know he was related to Reem's girl.

"At first he wasn't with it, until Ky told him to get out of her face for a little while." Bailey and Reem both laughed.

"Well whatever y'all wanna do, I'm down. I can't wait to see how y'all do in the A," I said while enjoying my food. Bailey seemed like a good person and I think I was gone be just fine staying here with her and my cousin.

TYREEM

Life was good for a real nigga these days. Money was rolling in, my family was straight, and most of all, I was so ready to marry my homie, lover, friend. Bailey and I came a long way, and right now shit is just perfect.

"What's up, sexy?" Bailey came in the room bringing me out of my thoughts.

"Nothing, sitting here thinking about how much I'm in love with my best friend."

"Is that right? I love you too, baby," Bailey cooed while she straddled me.

"Where're the twins at?"

"They've been bathed and put to bed. I wanted to spend time with my man before he went out for the night."

"Mmmmm, I think I like the sounds of that. So, what do you have planned?"

She got up and locked our door. Then she turned the Bluetooth speaker on, and put on *All These Kisses by* Tammy Rivera. Once the song came on, Bailey walked over to me, and started singing while dancing.

Day so hard, so much stress, life won't let up, boy just rest

Lay down and let me cover you in all these kisses

So much on your mind away from your head baby your worry-free in this bed

Go ahead and let me cover you in all these kisses........

I sat and watched Bailey like a hawk, while she sang, danced, and stripped out of her clothes. By the time the end of the song was finished, Bailey was ass naked and literally on top of me, kissing all over my neck and chest. While she was kissing the top part of my body, I was sliding out of my bottoms. At that very moment, I was like fuck the foreplay, all I wanted is to feel her insides. Once my bottoms were off, I pulled her up when I felt my mans poking at her opening. I slid her down on my dick.

"Shsssssss, Shit baby!" Bailey yelled.

"You good, Ma?"

"Yessssssss baby, I'm good now."

I guess she screamed like that because she needed to adjust to my size. No matter how many times we had sex, she was tight as hell, and needed to adjust to my size. While she bounced on my dick, I kissed and sucked on her titties. What drove me wild was when she sucked on her own nipples after me.

"Damn Ma, I love when you do that shit," I said. While Bailey was fucking me, I made sure I was fucking her ass right back. I felt my nut building up, but I wasn't ready to cum just yet.

"Slow down baby, ride it nice and slow for me."

"You want it nice in slow, daddy?"

She started riding me nice and slow like I asked her. Looking up at her was driving me wild. I couldn't take it anymore I flipped her little ass and kissed her lips before I ended up kissing her down below. After a couple of flicks of my tongue on her clit, Bailey was squirming all over the bed, trying to get away from the tongue.

"I'm cummin baby, I'm cummin!" Bailey yelled. See, when I eat her pussy, it doesn't take her long at all to cum. After I made sure she got her nut, I slid back into her and gave her a couple more long strokes before I felt my nut building up.

"Mmmmm, fuck Ma, I'm about to buss." After I bussed, I laid there for a second until I got my mind right.

"Baby get up, ain't you suppose be taking Taj out for a night."

"I know, give me a couple of minutes. You know what ya ass be doing to my body. I'm ready to take my ass to sleep now."

"Good, that's what I was trying to do, so when them hoes are in ya face, let them know ya nuts are already empty.Tell them ya wife took care of that before you left the crib."

"Ma, cut that shit out. You know I ain't got eyes for no one, but you."

"That's what I like to hear. I love you, Reem."

"I love you more, beautiful."

After kissing Bailey, I hopped up and went to shower. I had already told Jace, Samaad, and my right-hand Bro to meet us at the spot. I turned the water on and turned it to the temperature I like, then I jumped in. After I washed and rinsed a couple of times, I jumped out then dried off. I wrapped my towel around my waist and headed to my bedroom. Once I made it to my room, I looked at Bailey while she slept. I had the baddest chick in ATL. So, she never had to worry about me stepping out on her. We probably were going to bar hop or hit a club, so I decided on a pair of Robin Jeans and a regular white v-neck t-shirt. I knew I wasn't going anywhere special. I damn sure wasn't trying to look nice for nobody, my baby was lying in bed sleeping. I slid my feet in my black and white Jordan 12's and was ready to go. When I was fully dressed, I brushed my hair and sprayed some cologne on; then walked over to my bed and kissed Bailey. She stared up at me, and smiled.

"Baby, be safe out there. I love you."

"I'm always safe Ma, and I love you more." After leaving out the room I went to the boys' room and kissed them both on the forehead, then walked to Taji's room. I knocked on his door and he opened it right up.

"You finally ready nigga, I thought Bailey was keeping you in for the night." I chuckled at his crazy ass.

"Nah, she ain't like that. She doesn't mind me going out because I don't do it often."

"How long y'all been together?"

"We've been official for some years now, but we've been friends since we were fourteen.Yeah, when my parents died when I was sixteen that's when I moved to Jersey with y'all. Then when I turned eighteen, I came back to the A. When I moved back, Bailey was with her sucka ass baby daddy, but we still remained friends."

"Wow, that's a long time."

"Yeah it was, but I'm glad we started out as friends first. It's everything when you're in love with your best friend."

"That's what's up, I'm glad you're happy, cuz. But where's the twins' dad?"

"That's a whole nother discussion that we can talk about at another time."

"Oh ok, and I didn't know Bro was her brother."

"Bro is actually her twin brother. Bro and I were friends first."

"Oh ok I see, and I'm not gone ask what y'all into, because I already know. You know my dad didn't leave that part out."

Taji and I headed out the door to go link up with the fellas.

A half hour passed and we all were meeting up at the strip club. Bro had rented out a whole section for us. Everyone was in attendance, but I didn't understand why Jace had his chick with him. Little mama was beautiful, and innocent-looking. She didn't even seem like she was enjoying this environment.

"So, what's good Taj? I heard so much about you youngin," Bro said.

"I'm good my man, just glad to be in a different environment. I was getting sick of Jersey."

Jace burst out laughing. Taj looked at him and just brushed it off. For some reason Jace was acting funny tonight, and I didn't like it. Taj saw me about to say something, but he stopped me. I was gone listen to my cousin for tonight. He might have seemed quiet and like he wasn't about that life, but Taji was a sharpshooter and he could throw his hands. My uncle made sure we were trained to kill a muthafucka when need be. Bro ordered bottles and requested some ladies to our section. We were living it up.

"Yo Jace, what's ya girls name? You got her sitting here and didn't even introduce her to anyone," I asked.

"Why y'all gotta know who my bitch is?"

"My nigga, you better watch who the fuck you talking to. You've been beside ya self tonight, but I been letting you live," I barked. He sat his little punk ass down and didn't say shit else.

"What's ya name, little mama?" Taji asked.

The way Jace grilled him I knew he didn't like that shit at all, but little cuz didn't give a fuck and neither did I. Jace knew who the fuck I was, and his punk ass wasn't gone do shit.

"My name is Deja," she said just above a whisper. Something about her was off, but I just couldn't put my finger on it.

"I'm Taji, Deja. Nice to meet you, Ma." A little smile crept up on her face, and that shit angered Jace.

"Alright my nigga, that's enough trying to get to know my shawty."

Samaad was sitting there looking at Jace cracking up. Jace stood up and pulled his girl up out the seat then walked off. He didn't even say bye.

"Can one of y'all give me a ride home. This nigga just left and ain't tell me shit," Samaad asked.

"Yeah I got you," I said

Samaad and Jace were my foot soldiers. Jace's attitude sometimes got him in trouble. Samaad was a great worker and I could see him moving up in rank soon. We all continued to talk drink and enjoy our night, so I called one of the girls over so they could give my cousin a lap dance. He looked like a little kid in the candy store. I chuckled while I continued to take another shot.

"Yo cuz, pour me one," Taj said.

Shit, I poured that nigga a double shot. His ass was gone enjoy himself tonight. An hour or so passed by and Taj was done. Bro and I had to practically carry his ass to the car. I laughed the whole time, but as long as he had a good time, that's all that mattered to me.

"So, Reem what's up with youngin? We putting him on while he down here."

"Man, he ain't about this life, but Imma ask him. If not, I'll see if Bailey got something for him to do at the center."

"Yeah, I heard Ky and her talking the other day about needing a driver to take the girls around. And something about supplies being delivered. Shit, the pay was good too. I said I was about to drive that muthafucka." I burst out laughing.

"Well good looking Bro, I am going to bring him to the headquarters tomorrow to let him check it out. Maybe he might wanna do little shit for us, but I know music is his passion. I'm trying to get that studio up and running, then once it's finished, it's all his."

"That's what's up. I see you got mad love for the little homie," Bro said.

"Of course, that's my Unc's seed, the one who took me in when my family died. I'll give them the world."

"I hear that, but check this, let me get my ass home before Ky start blowing me. anytime after 3 a.m., she'll be in her truck out here looking for a nigga."

I started laughing at his ass while dapping him up. I watched Bro run to his car and hop in, we both pulled off at the same time. I was glad Samaad went home with one of his hoes because I didn't feel like making any stops. All I wanted to do was head home and slide up in my girl again and drift off to sleep.

DEJA

I hated that Jace made me go to the strip club with him. All I wanted to do was stay home. We had been together all day, so I was cool with the time we spent. I knew the night wasn't gone end well, he expected me just to sit and don't say anything. The whole time I was sitting there like a lump on a log not saying shit. Until handsome asked me my name. Truth be told, I had been eying him since he walked in. Something about him piqued my interest; once I heard him tell Bro he was from Jersey, I knew he was different. I knew once I told him my name and smiled at him, that would be the end of our outing.

Whap, whap, whap

"So you like smiling in other nigga's faces while you with ya man," Jace yelled while he delivered smack after a smack to my face.

We rode home in silence so I didn't think he as gone hit me. I knew he was pissed, but usually my beatings start right at the moment. So, I was shocked when he didn't drag my ass in the bathroom at the club and fuck me up, because he's done that before. I think it was something about him being with his boss, and being embarrassed by his boss, that angered him more.

"OUCH! Jace please stop hitting me, baby. You're going to leave marks on my face."

Usually he didn't hit me in my face because of how light I was, but the rest of my body was all bruised the fuck up.

"Shut the fuck up, Deja. That's why ya ass is getting beat now, because you don't know how to keep ya fucking mouth shut."

"Alright Jace, I'm sorry baby. I'm sorry."

My cries were never heard. His slaps went to punches, and now I was lying on the floor in a fetal position with him on top of me, throwing blow after blow.

"Now get ya dumb ass up and go take a shower, and get ya stupid ass in the bed."

It hurt me like hell to get up off the floor and took me forever to reach the bathroom. Once I made it to the bathroom, I locked the door and looked at myself in the mirror. My lip was bleeding and I had handprints on my face. Thank God I didn't have a black eye. Most of his punches were delivered to my lower part of my body. Usually after he beat me like this, he would sleep downstairs on the couch. After I hopped in the shower, I let the hot water run down my sore, bruised, and beaten body, while I cried and prayed to God that I would get out of the situation real soon. See, I've been going through this for a while and I think I'm finally getting sick of it. I love Jace, I do, and I'm having trouble understanding how I can I love someone that would hurt me like this. The loud banging on the bathroom door brought me out of my thoughts.

"Deja, are you almost done, baby?" *Here go that bipolar bullshit. Now this nigga sounds so sad like he didn't just fuck me up.*

"I'm coming out now, Jace."

"Alright, I'll be in the room waiting for you."

I hope to God he didn't want to have sex because I wasn't in the mood for that shit. After I dried off, I wrapped the towel around my waist, then headed in the room. Jace sat on the bed and watched my every move. I let the towel fall to my feet and laid down in the bed. He sat for a second not saying a word, but I could feel him staring at me from behind. I felt the bed move and then he appeared in front of me.

"I love you so much Deja, but you have to learn to keep ya mouth shut and respect me and this wouldn't happen," this nigga had a nerve to say before he kissed my lips and walked out of the room. Once again, he couldn't deal with what he did to me, so he went to sleep elsewhere. While I cried all night long, once again soaked in my own tears.

* * *

The sun shining in my room woke me up out of my sleep. When I looked at the clock, I saw it was 12 p.m. I never sleep this long, but for some reason I couldn't get myself to get up. I guess it could have been because of all the pain my body endured the night before. Hearing my phone ringing, I decided to get my ass up since it was on the other side of the room. Moving like the turtle I knew I was going to be today, I made it over to the dresser to grab my phone. When I saw it was no one but Jace, I wish I would have just laid my ass there.

"Hey baby, what's up?" he said before I got a chance to speak.

"Hey Jace, where are you?"

"I had some shit to do this morning, but I will be back soon. Are you hungry? Do you need me to bring you anything?"

"I'm not really hungry, Jace. I just wanna lay back down."

"Come on Deja baby, you have to eat something."

"I don't want anything, Jace. My body hurts and all I wanna do is go back to sleep."

"I'm sorry baby, I really am. Go ahead and lay down and I'll just bring you something to eat, and you can eat it when you feel up to it. I love you, now get you some rest."

I didn't even respond to him, all I did was hang the phone up and laid back in my bed. I needed my best friend. I hadn't seen or heard from her since Jace dragged me out of the club, and I missed her so much. I haven't called her yet, because I knew she didn't wanna talk to me. If she did, I figured she would have called by now. I felt myself going into a depressed state, so I just climbed back into my bed and cried myself back to sleep. An hour and a half done passed and I was still lying in the same spot I'd been in all night long, ass naked. The sound of my bedroom door opening brought me out of my thoughts.

"Hey baby girl, you still in here sleeping?"

"Yes, just don't feel good Jace, that's all."

"Alright, well I got you something to eat. If you get hungry just call me and I'll heat it up and bring it up to you."

"Ok, I'm gone to take a shower in a little bit then get up. Do you know where my Kindle is?"

"Yeah I put it in the drawer the other day after it was done charging."

Before Jace left to go back downstairs, he kissed my forehead and told me he loved me. Once he left the room, I got up, walked over to the drawer, and grabbed my Kindle. I needed something to take my mind off of what's been going on, so I decided to read a little. I used to read so much before Jace started feeling like I was ignoring him. I had to let him know this was the only thing I had to do since he wouldn't let me go anywhere. Then that's when he started being more understanding and left me alone when I was reading.

I powered my Kindle on and started looking through Shan Presents to see what new releases they had out lately. I came across a couple of new releases I knew I was gone go on a damn spending spree this week. The first two books I downloaded were *I Need You Bad* by Chanique J., and *Shawty Got Me Tryna Wife Her* by Rikenya Hunter. After I got my couple of books downloaded, I got my ass up and went to shower. Hopefully Jace would leave me alone.

JACE

Last night at the club I was so angry about Deja telling that nigga her name. Yeah, I know I should have left her home. But we had been spending time together, so when Bro hit me up to come out, I didn't wanna leave her home. I hate when I can't control my anger because then I can't keep my hands to myself. Now she's upstairs in this depression mode that I hate so much.

She won't even eat. She hasn't even told me she loves me when I say it to her. I know she's hurting, but all she has to do is stop making me mad all the time and she would be fine. I just ran upstairs to check on her again and she was still lying in bed with that sheet wrapped around her. Her face was still red from when I slapped her last night on both sides of her face. I usually don't hit her in her face because of her being so damn light. After I went to check on her, I ended up back downstairs, sitting in front of the TV, doing nothing. My ass was so fucking bored but I didn't feel like being out in the streets. A knock on my front door brought me out of my thoughts. I looked through the peephole and saw it was Samaad.

"Yo my nigga what are you doing here?" I asked while dapping him up.

"I went on the block and they told me you were out all morning then you left. So I figured you just did ya work early this morning."

"Yeah, I did. I wasn't really feeling being out there today."

"Where little sis at?"

"She upstairs, she not feeling good today."

Samaad had been my friend for years, so he knew Deja already. He was the only dude I let in my crib.

"Oh, ok. I saw her homegirl Tiombe last night after I left the club. Sade and I stopped at the Waffle House before we went to her crib. She asked about Deja and told me to tell her to call her."

"She doesn't need to call that hoe ass bitch."

"That's the only friend she has, Jace. Why are you always trying to treat her like she ya damn daughter and not ya girl. She's a whole grown ass woman. You gone keep the bullshit up and she gone leave ya stupid ass."

"Man, Deja ain't going no damn where. The only way she is leaving me is in a fucking body bag, and I mean that shit."

"Nigga, you wild as hell for saying some shit like that."

I hated listening to the shit that Samaad talked every time he came over here. He was like my brother, but he was always worried about Deja.

"Let me find out you want my girl the way you always to her defense."

"Come on man, don't start your bullshit. Deja is like a sister to me, just like you a brother to me. I just hate how you be treating her sometimes. She doesn't deserve that shit, man."

"If she fucking listen, she wouldn't be treated this way all the time."

"See, here you go talking that shit again like she's a kid. Come on let me beat ya ass in the game real quick before I go back on the block."

Samaad ain't said nothing but a word. I hurried and hooked the PS4 up and was about to kick his ass in some NBA 2k17. While I was behind the TV hooking the game up. I heard Samaad speak to Deja.

"Hey little sis, what's up?"

"What's up Maady, how you?"

Once she walked in the kitchen, I heard the microwave startup. Then ten minutes, later she came out with her food and a drink and she headed back upstairs. Samaad was staring at me with a mean ass look on his face.

"Man, why the fuck you looking at me like that?"

"Why the fuck you hit her like that, Jace. That shit is crazy man, I thought you said you weren't putting ya hands on her."

"Come on Samaad, you need to mind ya fucking business. Don't worry about what I do with my girl."

"That shit is foul, nigga. I'm out, but I'm letting you know now if she ever comes to me for help, Imma help her. I don't give a fuck about knowing you first, only bitch ass niggas hit on females," Samaad said and stormed out of my house.

I didn't give a damn about his attitude. What Deja and I went through was our business and no one else's. Since his punk ass left, I decided to play the game all by myself. While I was all into the game my phone alerted me that I had a text message. I picked it up and saw that it was Miko.

Miko: *Hey baby what's up with you.*

Me: *Hey Ma, I'm good how are you feeling.*

Miko: *I good just missing you. When are you coming to see me.*

Me: *I'll be through tonight since I ain't doing shit.*

Miko: *Alright I'll see you later.*

As I played the game I started to think about the shit that Samaad just said. I couldn't believe he said that shit to me, we go way back. We fucking brothers and he was gone to have her back, this shit was crazy. I felt myself getting angry, so I put my sneakers on and headed out the door. I didn't wanna go upstairs and take my anger out on Deja again, so I knew the best thing for me to do was to go outside somewhere until I was gone go to see Miko. I didn't even go upstairs and tell Deja I was leaving, I just grabbed my car keys and was out the door.

BAILEY

I was in my office gathering up some folders for the new girls that were coming in. My phone ringing brought me out of my thoughts.

"Hello, Lexi's Helping Hands, Bailey Monroe speaking."

"Hello Ms. Monroe my name is Lisa Fisher and I'm a social worker. I have a twenty-two-year-old mother and her two-year-old little girl, and I wanted to know if you had room and board for them?"

"I most certainly do, Ms, Fisher. When will they be arriving?"

"Well, the mother is still in the hospital, they want to keep her for a couple more days. She took a really bad beating this time."

"Is she safe there because if not we have our own staff for medical attention?"

"Well, we have police standing guard because they still haven't found her boyfriend yet. So, she should be fine."

"Where is her little girl at?",

"The baby is with her mother until she comes to y'all, and the police car is out in front of the mother's house as well."

"Ok. Ms. Fisher, can you give me her name, and the date of her release day and I'll have my transport pick her up from the hospital."

"Alright, Ms. Monroe, I'll email everything to you as soon as we hang the phone up."

"Ok, Ma'am and you have a nice day."

After I disconnected the phone, I sat at my desk for a second, thinking about the girl that was in the hospital.

"Hey baby, what you in here doing?" Ky asked when she walked in.

"Hey mama, what's going on. I just got off the phone with a social worker for a new client. The poor girl was in the hospital and has to stay for a couple of days. The social worker said he did a number on her this time. Ky, she's only twenty-two and she has a two-year-old daughter."

"That's sad, but I'm glad she'll be coming here for us to help her. It's like this shit never ends. Like, somewhere right now in the world there's someone getting abused. When it used to happen to me, I never knew it was so many people in the world going through the same situation as me. Shit, some people we get in here go through worse shit than me and you put together," Ky said.

"Girl I be wondering how the hell we can still hear these stories with our history."

"Girl, thank God for my therapist is all Imma say."

I laughed at Ky, but hell, she was telling the truth. The weekly counseling sessions really help me. By the way, my name is Bailey Monroe, and I'm co-owner of Lexi's Helping Hands with my sis-in-law Kylayda Monroe. Yes, her and my twin brother are married. I'm just waiting for her to pop out a niece or nephew soon. Ky and I decided to build Lexi's Helping Hands to help abused women. See, Ky and I had been through similar situations, now we wanted to help others get through it. I'll never forget what happened to me four years ago. My twins' father was upset because I had company over without asking him first. The crazy part was the company was my damn brother. I remember this shit so clear til this day. Hell, I even have nightmares sometimes and it's been years since it happened.

I had my eyes closed, putting my whole head under the water. I really didn't care about this dam hair at the moment, that's how good this was feeling. I felt a cold draft. The shower curtain was snatched open. I couldn't get my eyes open fast enough before the first lash hit my wet skin. I screamed so loud that if I had neighbors they would have heard me.

"Don't scream now bitch, you knew this was coming. You just gone come upstairs and go on with your night like you weren't fucking up all day."

He hit me again, sending another lash to my wet body. I was trying to guard my body the best way I could, but he was just swinging.

"Owwwwwww, you're hurting me, Leek. Please stop baby."

It seemed like every time I screamed, he hit me harder. I started to see blood running down the drain with the water I had open whelps all over my body. I didn't see them, but I sure as hell could feel my skin being ripped open with every lash. The hitting slowed down. By now, I was laying in the tub, almost out of it. Then here he comes, grabbing me by my hair, dragging me from the bathroom to the bedroom across the floor.

"Wake your ass up B you have to stay up for all the fun."

He started smacking my face to get my attention because I was in and out, almost unconscious. My naked body filled with blood, whelps, and rug burns from now being dragged across the floor.

"I don't know why you continue to do what Bailey wants to do all the time, never paying me any mind. Everything that I do to you is your own fault. You never want to be an obedient bitch," Leek screamed at me, right before he kicked me in my stomach.

I was in so much pain, I couldn't even scream anymore. Nobody could hear me anyway. I just laid there and took the beating. He beat me for hours, kicking, pulling my hair, smacks to the face, and he beat me some more with the belt. Then, he poured a bucket of scalding hot water on me every time he thought I was unconscious. I was gone for a second. My mind went to another place until I heard the front door slam, and brought me out of my thoughts. I wanted to get my phone to call for help, but I couldn't move. I guess I would be here on the floor until my nanny came in the morning.

"Sis, you good over there?" Ky asked while taking me out of my thoughts.

"Yes, I'm good boo."

"Alright, well Bro told me that Reem little cousin wanted to volunteer around here. I told Bro how much the job was paying and he laughed at me. He said Taji don't want no money, he just wanted something to do around here."

"Oh yeah, I talked to him already and he said he would do anything we needed him to do. He's a nice guy. I told Reem I really like him, and the twins are warming up to him."

"That's what's up. I'm sure we could use him for numerous things around here."

"Well, we have four new clients coming in this week. I have their rooms all set up and I'm trying to find a new guest speaker to come in to speak to the new classes," I said.

"You know what I was thinking, sis. Maybe one of us can tell our story."

"Yeah, that'll be good, and what else do we need to get together?"

"Nothing really, I went to Walmart and got the personals for the new clients," Ky said.

"We stay on point, sis. Do you know in a couple of weeks it will be two years since we've opened Lexi's Helping Hands."

"Yes, I know. Are we going to do another fun day like last year?"

"Yeah we can, that'll be great. You know the guys loved when we did it last year. They helped us so much."

Someone was knocking at our door, and we both said to come in at the same time.

"Hey Taji, what brings you by?"

"Reem told me it might be some stuff you ladies need help with around here and I figured I would come talk to you about it to see what I can do for y'all," Taji said."

"Hello beautiful. I'm Taji, and you are."

"Hello handsome, I'm Kylayda, your other boss," Ky said while putting her hand out for Taj to kiss it.

"Ump, Ump, Ump", I said while shaking my head. "You two better cut it out before Bro kill y'all."

"Oh, shit my fault. That's Bro?" Taji asked.

"Yup, this is Kylayda Monroe, Bro's wife."

"My fault Ms. Lady, I didn't mean any harm."

"I know you didn't, baby. You're such a gentleman. I like him, Bailey."

"Thank you, Ms. Ky. So ladies, tell me a little about y'all organization y'all got going on. I heard some from Reem and Bro, but I wanna hear from y'all."

"Well, Lexi's Helping Hands is a domestic violence center that we built to help the women that are abused seek shelter and guidance. Sometimes when they try to get away it's hard for them, so here we have everything they need. A lot of these women are actually hiding out."

"Wow, this is nice of you two to do. So, what made y'all do it?"

"We both were in an abusive relationship, and this center is named after Ky's baby girl that didn't make it, because of her being beaten up by her daughter's father while she was nine months pregnant."

"Damn, I'm sorry, Ms. Ky."

"It's cool Taj, I'm able to talk about it today. That's how I'm able to help so many people."

"Well I'm here to tell y'all this is a great thing y'all got going on."

" Enough about us, I heard you got some vocals."

"Yeah I can do a little something, something."

"Well let us hear what you got."

Taji started singing *Can You Stand The Rain* by New Edition and Ky and I were lost for words. His voice was so beautiful. He didn't even look like he was a singer. Once he finished the first verse, Ky and I started clapping.

"You better work it, boy," I said in amazement.

"You got some vocals on you. Maybe you can do a couple of shows for the girls sometimes. We try to have different types of things for them to do so they don't get bored here. You can do an amateur night type of thing," Ky said.

"That sounds cool I'm with it, so what else y'all need me to do around here?"

"You can start tomorrow, and I'll have a list of things you can do, and thanks so much for wanting to volunteer your time without being compensated."

"Ok cool! Bailey, and no thanks needed. I got more money than I know what to do with. Plus, I ain't doing shit. I don't mind helping out," Taji said.

After we gave Taji his paperwork, he filled everything out, then we gave him a tour around the building. Taji seemed like he would enjoy helping us around here. After he was done getting the rundown, he left out and I assured him that I would see him at the house later.

TAJI

After I met up with Bailey and Ky, I decided to go to my cousin's warehouse and check him and Bro out. Twenty minutes passed by and I was now pulling up to the warehouse. I shot Reem a text letting him know I was out front, so somebody could come let me in. By the time I got out the car and walked over to the door, the dude Samaad from the other night was letting me in.

"Hey my dude, what's up? Taj is ya name, right?"

"Yeah, that's me, and you Samaad right?" I asked while dapping him up.

"Yup, that's me. You enjoying it down here so far?"

"It's cool, anything is better than home right now. I needed a new atmosphere. Where Reem and Bro at?"

"They in the office. Come on, follow me."

This place was big as hell looking like a whole corporate building. From the outside, it looked just like a regular old warehouse; until you walked in this bitch. It was offices everywhere, elevators and shit. I was shocked at how they had it set up. Once we made to the office, Samaad knocked on the door, and Reem yelled, "come in."

"Yo cuz, what's up wit you?"

"Nothing really, I just came from seeing Bailey and Ky. Bro better always do right by her before I steal her."

"Yeah, ok youngin. I kill over that one," Bro assured me. Reem and Samaad started cracking up.

"Chill Killa, as long as you are doing right by her, you don't have to worry about me singing in her ear. You should have seen them both when I just serenaded them."

"Reem, get this little nigga before I beat his ass," Bro chuckled.

"Alright, let me leave you alone. So, what y'all got going on today?"

"Nothing much, we just made sure all our money is good. All our traps are supplied, and ain't no bullshit going on out in our streets. Samaad, what's up with Jace? I hadn't seen him since the other night," Reem asked.

"He came by the trap earlier and took care of his business then left. I ain't fucking with his punk ass right now," Saamad said.

"That nigga got issues, he doesn't even know me and I could feel the hate. Y'all don't need that nigga on y'all team. Any nigga that don't like somebody he doesn't know it's a jealousy thing. I tell y'all one thing, he better keep his shade to himself because he doesn't want these problems," I assured them. See, I might be the type to play around and sit quiet and don't say much, but I will kill me a mutha-fucka with no remorse."

"You good cuz, Jace know who you are. He wouldn't dare play with me like that."

"He better know before I steal his girl." They all burst out laughing.

"I see we gotta find you ya own pussy, before you take somebody else shit. These bitches like pretty ass singing niggas, too," Bro joked.

"Nah, let me stop fucking with y'all. Speaking of pussy, Reem Imma fly my friend Monae out here to spend the weekend with me next week."

"Nigga, you are flying pussy in town," Bro asked.

"Don't try to play me, Bro. If Ky were out of town, you wouldn't fly her into town?"

He thought for second before he answered. "Hell yeah, I would fly her fine ass into town."

"I knew you would, because hell, I would fly Ky ass into town."

"Youngin, you gone stop fucking playing with me about my wife, before I kick ya ass," Bro barked.

"Alright man, Imma chill. What else y'all doing for the day?"

"I'm taking Bailey and the boys out today, and she doesn't know it yet," Reem said.

"I was chilling in the crib with Ky today since we've been so swamped with work," Bro said.

"Well damn, where does that leave me?" I asked.

"You can chill with me, I could show you some more of the A, if you want to?" Samaad inquired.

"I'm with that, my man."

"Do me a favor Samaad, while you got Taj with you. Go past all the traps and make sure they straight. Then you can do you. Bro and I were discussing bringing you up in rank. Instead of you babysitting a trap, I'll have you checking on them, doing rounds. Meaning you pick up money and drop off product. If you want, Taj can help with that, if he doesn't mind."

"I'm good with that cuz, whenever I'm not volunteering at the center," I assured Reem.

"Wow, thanks y'all, I really appreciate that," Samaad marveled.

"No thanks needed nigga, you stay putting in work, and dropping everything you're doing to come see what we need. Your pay goes up a lot as well, but we will talk about that later," Reem assured Samaad.

"Well shit, I'm hungry Samaad. Where's our first stop? Is it near some good food?"

We dapped Reem and Bro up, then I let them know I was leaving my car, and hopping in the car with Samaad. Samaad seemed like a really cool dude ever since I first met him. So, I knew we would click.

DEJA

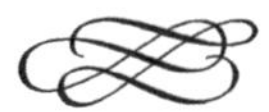

"Jace wake up, I need to get to Walmart to get some personals."

"Come on Deja, just let me sleep a little longer. I'm tired Ma, I had a long night."

I had been trying to wake him up for the last hour and a half. When I tell y'all, I'm so fucking annoyed. I have my own fucking car and he still wants to take me everywhere.

"If you just let me go by myself, I wouldn't have to wake you up. Walmart is right around the corner, Jace."

It took him a little while to answer, but he eventually told me to go ahead and go.

"Go ahead Deja, but if I wake up and you not here, I'll find ya little ass and kill you."

The way he sounded when he said that was so cold, so I knew he meant business. When I got up to grab the car keys, I noticed his phone was going off, and the name Amiko was flashing across the screen. I wasn't gone answer it, but I was gone damn sure check the call log and text messages to see who this Amiko was. Leaving my phone and picking up his was what I did.

See, we had the same phone and we often made the mistake of

grabbing each other's phone. Once I made it to the car, I hopped in and started the car up and drove to the closest Walmart which was about ten minutes from our home. When I got to the parking lot, I sat for a while and opened his phone up. Yeah, I knew Jace's code. He didn't know I knew, because I never used it. I knew he cheated, that's why I never really looked for anything. I don't know what made me wanna look this time. Once I opened his text messages, my heart broke when I came across the pregnancy test. The tears started rolling down my face instantly. Not only was this bitch pregnant, but it seems that they have been dealing with each other a long time. I knew what I was about to do would get me an ass beating, but I needed to know for my own sanity how long has this been going on. I hit the call button to call to dial her number.

"Hey baby, I was waiting for you to call. Last night was everything."

"So, how long you and baby been messing around?" She paused for a second before she actually caught on.

"Look little girl, don't call me questioning me. Ask your man."

"I asked you and trust me Imma ask my man too, but it's always two sides to a story."

"Listen little mama, I ain't got time to be sitting on this phone fussing with you over Jace no-good ass. So like I said before, talk to ya man and let him tell you what it is you trying to find out."

Of course she wouldn't talk to me, but the truth was they had something going on. Now, me ask Jace what was going on I would never do. But I knew she would tell him I called her and all hell was gone break loose. Making sure to erase the recent calls and text messages so that way it would give me some time, I wanted to just drive far away from here and go somewhere that I wouldn't be found. Enough was enough, and I needed to find a way to get away from Jace. I wiped my tears, then got out the car so I can go into Walmart. The news I just found out had me dragging in the store. My feelings were so fucking hurt. This nigga took everything away from me and made me stay in the house while he's out doing him. I grabbed me a cart and headed to get some toothpaste, deodorant, pantyliners, feminine wipes and spray. Then while walking over to women's department to get me some comfortable pajama sets, I heard someone calling my name. I turned to see who it was and it was Samaad with Mr. Sexy that was from Jersey following him.

"Hey Maady, what's up?

"What you doing here, sis? Where's Jace at?"

"He's home sleeping, and I needed some things, so he told me to come get them." Maddy knew how Jace was, that's why he asked.

"Oh ok, well you got my number sis. Call me if you ever need anything." I thought him saying that was kind of strange, but I knew he meant it.

"Well if it isn't Little Ms. Deja. Hey there, beautiful," Taji beamed.

"Hello Taji, how are you?"

"I'm great since I saw you and you remember my name," he said while smiling at me.

"What y'all two doing?" I asked.

"Handling business for Reem's girl," Maady told me.

"Alright, well it was nice seeing y'all. I gotta go before Jace has a fit," I said while walking away.

I could feel Taji's eyes on me, so I turned around and winked at him and he smiled. I knew I wasn't right flirting with that boy, but something about him had me intrigued. When I had everything I needed, I hurried and ran to the register and paid for my things. I needed to hurry up and enjoy my time before he woke up and ole girl told him I contacted her. Once he found out I knew my ass was as good as beat. I know y'all trying to figure out why I just don't leave, but it's easier said than done. I have nothing of my own, everything that I had comes from him. It's like he had a tracking device on my ass whenever I went anywhere, he found me. After making it to the register and paying for my things, I hurried and left out the store. Once I found my car, I hopped in and took off, heading back to the hell hole. Ten minutes went by and I was pulling back up in front of our home. Jace was standing at the door waiting for me. When I got out and went to the trunk he met me and grabbed all the bags.

"What took you so fucking long, Deja?" This nigga was just

sleeping and didn't wanna get up and take me, but wanna know what took me so long.

"I'm sorry baby, the store was so crowded."

"You better be glad you came back when you did. I was about to come look for ya ass."

"Jace, I was coming right back. If you feel that way, you should have got up and taken me."

Whap, Whap

"Who the fuck you think you are talking to, Deja? I swear you and that fucking mouth. Why the fuck can't you just keep ya mouth shut. Since you don't wanna keep it shut, when you get ya ass in the house, get on ya knees, so I can put this dick in ya mouth."

After I looked around to make sure no one was outside, I ran in the house and did as I was told. I was so glad no one was outside to witness Jace slapping the shit out of me. As I entered the house he walked in behind me, slamming the door shut.

"Where the fuck you going? I said get the fuck on ya knees," Jace barked. I stopped in my tracks and got on my knees, facing him. He dropped the bags to the floor and whipped his dick out.

"Show me what that mouth can do, and you better do it right." I licked the head of his dick before I got started. I guess I was taking too long for Jace's liking. He rammed his dick in my mouth, causing me to gag.

"If you throw up on my shit, I'm gone beat the shit out of you after you swallow my seeds. Now suck my dick the way I like it done," Jace roared.

I continued to suck him off the way he loved it, hoping he would cum any minute. Usually it didn't take me long to make Jace nut but I guess it was taking long cause I wasn't feeling it. Once he started fucking my face in a fast motion, I knew he was about to reach his peak.

"That a girl do it just like that. You ready to swallow these babies," Jace asked.

Looking into his eyes, I nodded my head yes. As soon as I nodded my head, Jace was shooting his seeds down my throat. Once he was finished, he wiped his dick off on my shirt and put it back in his pants. When I went to stand up, he looked at me with a mean scowl on his face.

"Did I tell you to get the fuck up."

I eased my way back down on the floor until he told me to get up. Jace headed upstairs, I guess to take care of his hygiene. My legs were starting to get sore from being on this damn floor. I felt the tears building up in my eyes, but I didn't want them to fall. After about twenty minutes, Jace was coming downstairs fully dressed and smelling like cologne. He grabbed his car keys and was headed out the door. I know this nigga ain't about to walk out the door and leave me sitting here like this.

"Oh shit Dej my fault, Ma. You can get up now, and make sure my dinner is made when I get back." He walked over to me, pulled me in for a hug, and kissed my forehead.

"Jace wait, here goes your phone. I grabbed the wrong on earlier," I said, handing him his phone. I wanted him to leave and stay gone for hours. Shit, hopefully he didn't come back until tomorrow.

"I love you, Ma," was the last thing he said while walking out the door. The pain I endured while dealing with Jace was starting to be too much, but I didn't know how to leave him. Is it crazy for me to love this man the way I do?

JACE

I hadn't been really playing the trap houses like that lately; I'd just been doing my job than being out. I noticed I hadn't talked to Samaad in a minute, so I figured I would go by the trap and check him out. This was the third one I had been to and Samaad wasn't there.

"Yo Quan, what's up with Samaad? Where he been at lately?"

"I heard he wouldn't be in the traps liked that, he just collect the money and drop off product now. That nigga done moved up in the world. What's up wit y'all two?"

I couldn't believe this shit. How Reem gone let this nigga move up and he met him through me? If anything, I should have had that position before him. But I ain't gone trip, I can't wait to see him to congratulate him. Once I chopped it up with Quan for a little bit longer and handled some business, I headed out the trap and ran right into Samaad and that nigga Taj. I don't know what it was about this nigga, but I just wasn't feeling him at all.

"Hey Jace, what's good, my boy," Samaad said while dapping me up.

"Yo bro what's good with you. Why you haven't been to the crib?"

"I've been out here making moves."

"I heard, congratulations on moving up." Even though I wasn't happy about it, I still needed to show some type of love.

"What's up, Jace?" Taji said and I didn't speak. I just kept talking to Samaad.

"Yo my nigga, what did I ever do to you?"

I chuckled before I responded. "Nigga, I don't know you not to like you, but I don't do newcomers, that's all."

"Chill Jace, he's Reem blood. Why are you tripping?" Samaad inquired.

"I don't care who family he is."

"Listen here Jace, you ain't never got to like me because I don't have to deal with you. Don't let this quietness fool you, I can buss my guns and throw these hands. So, watch ya fucking mouth when you talking to me. I don't do disrespect, and I've killed for less, so watch how the fuck you talk to me."

"Come on T, man let's be out. Jace, I'll get up with you tomorrow," Samaad assured me while pulling pretty away.

I wasn't strapped, so I wasn't gone say anything to his punk ass anyway. Walking away and heading to my car, a nigga was pissed off and didn't feel like doing shit, but get fucked. I pulled out my phone and dialed Miko's number before I pulled off.

"Hey beautiful, what's good with you?"

"What do you want, Jace?"

"Wooh Ma, what's with the attitude?"

"You need to keep ya bitch in control."

"For one, you need to watch ya fucking mouth when you are talking to me."

I didn't know what was wrong with everybody today. It seemed like everyone wanted to come at me sideways today.

"Jace I ain't that bitch, you better watch who the fuck you talking to."

I didn't know what the hell she was talking about, but I wasn't feeling her attitude. That's when it dawned on me that Deja got our phones mixed up earlier. I wonder if she took my shit on purpose, or did she really pick up the wrong one. Even if that was the case her little ass had no business going through my fucking phone. Now I had to go kiss up to Miko to get her out of her feelings, then I was gone home to beat Deja's ass. I was gone teach her to mind her fucking business and stay out of my phone.

After about twenty minutes, I was now pulling up in front of Miko's house. I parked my car then hopped out; I knew she was in there because her car was parked. Using my key, I walked in and she was in the kitchen at the sink washing dishes. She was so busy shaking her ass to the music that was playing she didn't even hear me walk in. I walked up behind her and grabbed her waist and she nearly jumped out of her skin.

"OH MY GOD! Why would you scare me like that, Jace?"

"Shut ya punk ass up and give me a kiss." She turned around and kissed my lips. She let out a soft moan as I grabbed her ass and squeezed it while we kissed.

"Stop Jace, I'm supposed to be mad at you right now." Her saying that reminded me of her smart mouth a little while ago.

"I almost forgot. Who the hell were you talking to Miko?"

"You nigga, learn how to keep ya bitch in check, and you wouldn't have to worry about me talking to you like that."

Before I knew it I slapped the shit out of Miko. She grabbed her face and looked at me with a death stare. After her little stare off, she turned to the sink like she was gone continue to wash the dishes.

"Don't you ever call her a bitch again. I'm the only one that's allowed to call my bitch out of her name. Do you understand, Amiko?" She didn't say shit and I didn't like the way she was ignoring me. So I walked up behind her and grabbed her hair.

"I hear you baby. Please, let my hair go."

Once I let her hair go, I walked over to the fridge to get me a water. Then I walked upstairs to shower and lay across her bed. I couldn't wait until she got done so she could come fuck me to sleep. A half hour had passed and I was now showered and waiting on Amiko. Her house was empty, so you could hear everything. I heard the music go off, so I assumed she was on her way upstairs. I was lying with my back, facing the door.

"It's about time you got up here what the hell took you so long?"

She didn't say anything, but I felt movement on the bed, which let me know she was climbing in. Once I felt the cold steel on the back of my neck, I ain't even gone lie, I was scared shitless.

"Get the fuck up and get out of my house. I don't know what you do to that bitch you got at home, but I will not allow a muthafucka to put his hands on me. My parents didn't raise me that way. I was taught that only bitch ass niggas hit on females, and make sure you grab all your shit, because that was the first and last time you'll ever touch me. Hurry the fuck up before I shoot ya ass right in the dick where it hurts."

I jumped up and put my clothes on, then I went to her closet and got my duffle bag out that I had over here in case I couldn't make it home. I tell y'all no lie, I was dressed and ready to go in about five minutes. As soon as I had all my shit, I was headed out the bedroom door.

"I'm sorry for putting my hands on you, Miko."

"Nigga save that shit for somebody else. Hurry up and get the fuck off my property."

Miko followed me out of her room all the way out the front door, making sure I left. Once I made it to the car, I was glad God spared me my life. When I made it in the car, I started it up and sat for a minute before I pulled off.

"Oh, you must need me to make ya ass move faster," I heard Miko screaming at me.

I looked out the rearview mirror and this crazy bitch had her gun pointed at me, and she let off a couple of shots. My back window shattered and my ass peeled off quick as hell. I guess that goes to show I can't handle every female as I do Deja.

TAJI

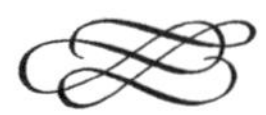

"So bro, what's up with you and little mama? You always got a sad look on ya face when you see her. I peeped it at the club the other night and I peeped it again today."

"Nothing man, she's good peoples and I think she deserves better than Jace."

"Well I don't really know her or dude, and I can tell she needs better. How do you know ole boy?"

"Jace and I grew up together. He's not like he used to be, though. He changed big time, and I don't know why."

"Well that nigga got jealousy and envy in his eyes. Don't trust him, bro."

"Man, you don't have to tell me that, I already know what it is. He really hates that you and I are getting cool."

Samaad and I were pulling up to the center and I was going in to take Bailey the stuff I got from Walmart.

"Come on, let's go." Samaad got out of the car looking at the center like he was amazed.

"What type of center is this?"

"It's a domestic violence center."

"Oh word? This shit is in the cut. I never knew we had one in our city."

"I think that's the reason they put it here so that it won't be noticeable. See, they shelter the girls and their kids here to hide them from their abuser, then they help them find jobs and houses. Showing them that there is life at the end of being abused."

"Yo, this is dope man, I like the whole idea of it."

"Right, that's what I said when I first came here." Once Samaad and I made it inside, Ky was at the desk answering the phones.

"Now what is the boss doing sitting up front answering the phones?"

"Taji, shut up boy, my secretary needed to go to lunch. Hey Maady, how are you doing? It's been a minute since I saw you."

"Hey Ky, what's up. That's because I haven't been over y'all crib in a minute."

"Right, I asked Bro about you and Jace the other night and he said y'all were good."

"Yeah. I'm good, I don't know about Jace, though. He hasn't been messing with me lately. All the years I've known you and I never knew y'all owned this place. Taj told me what y'all do here. That's what's up, I admire this."

"Awww, thank you, baby. I enjoy helping and saving lives."

"Well I just came by to drop the stuff off for Bailey, and I'm trying to get the amateur night thing going on. We should be able to host one in a couple of weeks, ok."

"Alright Taji, and thanks again for helping us out around here. We really appreciate it."

"No problem Ky, I told y'all I'll always support. This is for a good cause." After I got finished bussing it up with Ky, Samaad and I left out.

"Alright bro, what else do we have on the agenda?" Samaad asked.

"Nothing else, I was gone head back to Reem crib, and just chill."

"Well I guess I'll head on in myself. Since I ain't got shit else to do."

An hour had past and I had dropped Samaad off and now I was

back at Reem's crib relaxing. My phone was ringing, bringing me out of my thoughts.

"Hey sexy, what's up?" Monae cooed in the phone.

"Hey Ma, what's good with you?"

"Nothing much. I can't wait to come see you Friday."

"Can't wait to see you either, Ma. So, what you been up to?"

"Going to school, that's it. My dad keeps fussing about me getting a job, but why do I have to when we have money."

"I keep telling you Monae, that you need to get out here and learn how to make ya own money. Your pops just trying to show you how to do ya own thing. He can't take care of you for the rest of your life."

"He won't have to, that's what I have my future husband for."

I knew she was talking about me, but I wasn't listening to her ass she better go on ahead somewhere. See, this is why I was falling out of love with Monae. I know y'all probably wondering why I still deal with her. I guess y'all could say she was something to do until I found my Queen. Not really wanting to get into an argument with Monae, I didn't even respond to her statement. Deciding to change the subject was the best thing to do.

"So, you missing me like crazy?"

"Yes, I wish I could stay longer than the weekend, but I can't afford to miss any classes. Daddy said if I don't pass this semester, he's cutting me off."

"What's been going on with you, Monae? I thought we talked about you and school."

"I know Taj, I'm trying to do better. I think it has a lot to do with missing you."

After that bogus ass shit she just said I knew it was time for me to hang up. I would deal with her ass when she made it here.

"Baby, I'm gone call you back as soon as I go see what my daddy wants."

Her dad probably wasn't even calling her, but I didn't care. I was about to hang up with her ass anyway. After I hung my phone up, I plugged it up to charge, and then I just continue to lay down. A nigga was tired and needed to get a little nap in.

SAMAAD

After Taji dropped me off at home, I heated me up some leftovers, then sat down to watch TV. Thoughts of Deja came to mind, and I hoped she was good. I'd been having bad vibes since I last saw her. I knew Jace choked her up and mugged her, but I never knew him to give her black eyes. Shit, I've yoked up a couple of chicks in my time, but if they got me to the point where I wanted to kick their ass, I would leave first.

By the way, I'm Samaad Smith and I was born and raised in Atlanta Georgia. I'm an only child and it's just my favorite lady and me, which is my mother. Never knew my dad, and my mom did a damn good job raising me. Minus the street shit. Yeah, we argued plenty of times about that, but I promised her I would turn my life around for the better before I had a family of my own, and she rolled with that. As soon as I was about to dig in my plate, there was a knock at my door. This was odd, because I didn't do company like that. I peeked out the peephole and saw it was Tiombe.

"Hey Ma, what brings you by?"

"I've been thinking about you since the last time I saw you, so I figured I'd stop by. Well, are you gone let me in?"

"Oh shit, my fault. I'm just shocked to see you here, that's all."

I moved to the side and let her enter my home. Tiombe and I slept together a while ago, but she was a little too wild for me. So, I never thought it would be more than us just fucking around.

"What you in here eating?"

"Some shit my mom cooked for me. You know I don't have a girl so, my mama be cooking for me, or I eat out."

"Well why don't you have a girl, Samaad?"

"Haven't found one that ain't on the bullshit, and what brings you over here."

"I've missed you, Sammad," Tiombe said just above a whisper. I looked at her with the side eye, not knowing where the fuck that came from.

"Where is all this coming from, Ma? We've fucked around in the past, but I never known you to be serious."

"I just took it for what it was, Samaad. All we did was fuck when we were out clubbing and shit like that. I didn't wanna be like I wanted more, and it wasn't what you wanted, then my feelings would be hurt."

"Tiombe, you were known as the party girl and you knew good and got damn well I wouldn't have my girl always partying."

"Samaad, I was doing single shit because that's what single people do. Now if you wanted more out of what we had going on, why wouldn't you say something to me?"

"So that's what you popped up over here for? To tell me how you really feel about me."

"When I saw you last time, you've been on my mind ever since."

"What if I had company?"

"Then I would have left, and if you want me to leave now, I will."

"Nah, you good Ma. I would never make you leave. Have you saw Deja lately?"

"Not ever since her bitch ass nigga threw me on the ground."

"Wait, when this shit happen?"

"Like a week or two ago. I can't stand that nigga, he is so fucking controlling and jealous. Ever since she been with him, I stay away. That's my sis and I love her dearly, but I can't deal with his simple ass.

I hope she is not letting him beat her ass, because he definitely has signs of an abusive ass nigga."

Hearing her say that, I knew Deja must didn't tell her, and I felt like it wasn't my place, so I kept my mouth shut.

"Wow! I can't believe that nigga, and don't go over her house without me."

"I don't go over there. I miss my BFF, but I just can't do her dude."

"Yeah, Jace has been on one lately. I hadn't even been kicking it with him in a minute. Oh shit, my fault Ma, are you hungry?"

"Nah I'm good, I ate before I came over."

"Oh ok, well what you wanna do tonight? You wanna go out or just chill inside and watch TV."

"We can stay in, I don't feel like going out tonight."

I sat and stared at her for a second Tiombe was beautiful. She was on the dark side, which was fine with me. I loved my women dark. Her body wasn't the body these niggas died for today, but it was fine with me. She had small boobs and a little-plumped ass with a flat belly. I loved the long braids she was rocking right now.

"It's rude to stare, you know."

"My fault Ma, just admiring your beauty. Is something wrong with that?"

"It's nothing wrong with that at all," Tiombe said while smiling. I put my plate down and got up and grabbed her hand and pulled her over to sit next to me.

"So, be real with me, Ma. Tell me the real reason why you just popped up over here."

"I told you, the last time I saw you put me in my feelings. I've always known I wanted you, I just didn't know how to tell you."

I didn't know if I was buying what Tiombe was saying, but I was gone see where her head was really at. Tiombe and I sat, talked, watched TV and chilled for the rest of the night. I wasn't used to this, but hey, I didn't mind it. It felt kind of funny sitting and talking without wanting to bend her little ass over. I knew I probably could, but I wasn't on that tonight I really wanna give this shit a try, if she's serious.

TYREEM

"Yo bro, have you heard from Jace?" Brodie asked.

"Nah, why what's up?"

"This nigga still ain't come back from making that run for me. I knew I should have gotten Samaad to do it."

"That nigga been slipping lately. I'm about to give his ass some walking papers. We got plenty of soldiers that would love to take his spot," I barked. As soon as those words left my mouth, this nigga came strolling in like he had an attitude.

"Nigga, you don't just walk in my fucking office, you knock first."

"Come on Reem, man the door was open."

"I don't give a damn, and where the hell you been?"

"I was handling business for Bro."

"Nigga, what took ya ass so fucking long, and all my cash better be here," Bro barked.

"Now, here you go. Why y'all coming at me like this?"

"Look Jace, you've been around for a minute, but what's really good with you? It's like you slipping on your duties."

"Do you want me to be honest with you?"

"Hell yeah nigga, be honest."

"Well first of all, I don't like how shit is going around here. How y'all gone move Samaad up in rank before me. I grew up around y'all niggas in the same hood. Y'all met him through me."

Bro looked up at this nigga with a raised eyebrow. I guess he was trying to see how I was gone handle this. Believe it or not, I'm the crazy one out of the bunch. I don't do disrespectful shit, and jealous niggas die.

"First and foremost, are you questioning my choice?" I grimaced with so much anger.

"Come on Reem man, calm down. You told me to be honest."

"Tell me Jace, what other reasons do you think I should have given you the job?"

He sat there with nothing else to say; I didn't know if he was scared or he just didn't have an answer.

"That's what the fuck I thought. Reem, he doesn't have shit to say. Listen little nigga, only people who are putting in real work get moved up," Brodie let Jace's ass know.

"You know what Jace you seem like you jealous my man, and we don't have room for jealous niggas on our squad."

"What you talking about, Reem? I won't be able to live without working for you."

"Leave him on Reem, just put that nigga back down as a trapper. He gotta stand on the corner day in and day out, bussing traps. If he can handle that without any fuck-ups, then he will get his job back."

Jace just sat there with a mean look on his face, but we didn't give a fuck. We did what we wanted to do, and who was gone check us.

"Give Brodie his package and you can leave. Oh yeah, and you got the graveyard shift."

He handed Brodie the bag and then he stormed out of the office. Bro and I bust out laughing, that nigga was recalling gone be in his feelings now.

"He not gone last out there. I'll give him a week or two, tops."

"I know, but I knew he wasn't gone turn the job down. How else was he gone eat? We gone need to watch out for his ass though, he got jealousy in his eyes."

"Yeah, I peeped that."

While we talked, Brodie pulled out the money that was in the bag Jace gave him and counted it to make sure it all was there. After he was done counting, he sat for a while, staring in a daze.

"What's good Bro, you've been doing that a lot lately."

"I've been doing what a lot lately?"

"Come on man, you know what I'm talking about. You've been quiet and not talking much and working. Nigga, we are the bosses, we barely have to put work in but you have been lately."

"Ky been having trouble getting pregnant. So, we went to the doctor's and got all types of tests done. They even checked me. I was good. But they think when she lost Lexi, it might have messed her up and we might not be able to have any babies, Reem." Hearing him say that broke my heart.

"Damn Bro, I'm sorry to hear that. But y'all can always adopt, man."

"I know, but this shit has my wife all fucked up right now. She goes to work and acts like nothing going on, holding that shit in all day. Then when we get home, she's up crying all night. She hasn't even told Bailey yet."

"Damn, that shit's crazy, but y'all gone get through this."

"I keep trying to tell her I love her and she doesn't need to feel less of a woman. We can adopt. She says that's not the same as giving me a life that has my blood running through its veins. Then she says to me the other night 'don't be out here cheating on me Brodie, if you feel the need to cheat, leave me first'. I swear on my sis and the boys, Ky not being able to give me a baby doesn't change the love I have for her."

"I know it doesn't man, but she's a woman and this shit hurts like hell. You just have to be strong for the both of y'all."

"I'm trying, but I feel like she's pushing me away."

"She just in her feelings, Brodie. Just give her some time."

"I am. She can have all the time she needs. But pushing me away ain't happening, so I hope that's not what her plans are."

"I wonder why she hasn't talked to Bailey about it. She might need to vent to make her feel a little better."

"I have no idea. I asked her why she hasn't talked to her and she snapped on me about not wanting nobody to know her business. So please, whatever you do, don't say anything. Let her tell it herself."

"You got my word. I would never put ya business out there." I could see that this shit had Bro all fucked up, and hope it gets better for them soon.

"When we gone show Taji the studio?"

"I thought this weekend. I wanted them to put the finishing touches on it."

"Yo, I think that's great what you are doing for him."

"That's my little homie. I'll do anything for my little cousin. His daddy not gone be too pleased, but hey, not everybody gotta be in the streets the make money."

"Shit, I hear that. Well, let me get ready to get out of here. I'm trynna take my wife to dinner if she's in the mood."

"Yeah, I need to be getting out of here myself. Bailey wanna go to the movies to see *True to the Game*."

After Bro and I talked a little more, we locked our office up and headed out for the evening. The thought of what he and Ky were going through came across my mind and all I could do was shake my head and wish them the best.

BAILEY

I was sitting in my office getting ready to meet with my new client. She was just now getting out of the hospital. While I was cleaning off my desk, I heard a knock at the door.

"Come in," I yelled across the room. A beautiful young lady walked in. She had bruises on her face, but she was still beautiful. Walking in holding onto her leg, she had the prettiest little princess.

"Hello Ms. Monroe, I'm Rayne and this is my baby girl, Eva."

"Well, hello Rayne, how are you love."

"I'm ok now that I'm here." Once she started talking, I sat down at my desk.

"Go ahead and have a seat, Rayne. If you want me to, I can call and have one of the girls pick up Eva and take her to the daycare."

She hesitated at first, but I assured her that we could see her on the monitor from here. I paged Ms. Helen from the daycare and had her get the baby. The daycare wasn't far from my office, so she was knocking on my door in about five minutes.

"Rayne, this is Ms. Helen, our daycare supervisor."

"Hello Ms. Helen, if you have any problems with Eva you can bring her back."

"I'm sure she'll be fine. It's plenty of other kids in there and toys, she'll be just fine," Ms. Helen said while picking Eva up.

"How old is she?"

"She's two and she's my world."

"I have three-year-old twin boys."

"Oh really, how do you manage with twins?"

"It's a lot, but I wouldn't trade motherhood for anything in the world. So Rayne, tell me why you're here. I know it's going to be hard to talk about, but the first step to moving on is dealing with what happen and learning from it. Your story could one day save another's life like mine does all the time."

"Terell and I have been together since we were eighteen. I thought he was my everything until I turned twenty and moved in with him. After a couple of months of living together, the beatings started. I was gone leave, then when we found out I was pregnant with Eva. He promised he would stop, and I believed him." As soon as she said that part, the tears started to fall down her face.

"Well, you don't have to worry about him anymore, Rayne. You will be safe here. So, what caused him to hurt you this time?"

"He's having trouble keeping a job and it makes him angry. He doesn't want me to work, but I always tell him that me working can help us. He made me stop going to college. I had a full scholarship and I messed that up because of him. My mother has disowned me for dropping out of school. Ms. Monroe, I need a better life for Eva."

"Well if that is what you want Rayne, we are here to help. It'll take time but we will do all we can here at Lexi's Helping Hands to help. We do have rules and regulations here, but one of them is not keeping you here. We never want y'all to feel like we are keeping you here against your will. If you happen to wake up and wanna leave, fine, do you. Just make us aware. No one can come here to visit you. We try to keep you all safe. We don't wanna risk your boyfriend finding our location. There's Daycare for Eva and there are jobs you can sign up for if you would like. Also, we do online college courses. We always make it so that you're not bored here. Once you get used to the swing of things around here, you'll be just fine. When we feel like you're doing well enough to leave, we help you relocate. We prefer you move away far, but if you don't want to, we help you make the proper moves where as though your mate will never hurt you again. If you need any personals, let us know. We also have hairdressers and a nail salon in here."

"Wow! I never knew places like this existed."

"We're probably the only place that exists like this."

"You look young Ms. Monroe, what made you wanna come into a business like this?"

"Well Rayne, just like you, I have a story to tell. I'm actually co-owner of this place with my sister-in-law. The whole place was her idea, and when she found out about my abuse, she told me her story and asked me to go into business with her. It's been a success ever since. You'll meet Ky as well. Everyone calls her Ms. Ky, since we share the same last name."

"You ladies have an excellent thing going on here. I just hope I'm ready for this. Ms. Monroe, why do I feel sad for leaving him. It's not normal to love someone that hurts me. What is wrong with me? " I could see in her eyes that she wasn't sure of her choice.

"Those are questions I used to ask myself all the time, Rayne. Never think you're dumb or stupid; you just need help. While you're here, we assure you that you will get the proper help that you need as long as you let us help you. I have counselors that come in twice a week to meet with each girl. Is that something that you will be interested in while you're here?"

"Yes Ms. Monroe, I'm interested in everything you have in store for me."

"Alright, well I'll put you down to start next week, so that way you'll get both days in. Now that's all for today, Rayne. If you have any questions about anything, don't hesitate to stop by my office."

"Ok Ms. Monroe, I will be keeping in touch."

Once Rayne left out my office, I closed the door and sat in my thoughts for a little bit. She was so young and going through all of this, and to hear her mother disowned her. I hoped and prayed that we helped her to the best of our ability.

"Hey sis, what's up?" Ky asked walking into the office.

"Hey mama, I just got done a meeting with Rayne King. The one I told you about that has the two-year-old daughter."

"Yeah, I remember her. How is she?"

"She's alright considering what she's been through. I'm just not sure she's ready for our help, but you know how we do. We'll try to help her as much as we can."

I looked over at Ky and she seemed to be in a zone. Lately, she just has not been herself, but she keeps telling me she's ok.

"What about you? You haven't been looking good lately."

Ky hesitated for a minute, next thing I knew, tears started running down her face. I jumped up and ran over to her and pulled her in for a hug.

"Bailey, why did this have to happen to me?"

"What's the matter, baby? What are you talking about?" I started rattling off questions because I needed to know what was wrong with my sister.

"I can't give Brodie babies. What kind of wife am I if I can't birth any babies for my husband? He's gonna fall out of love with me and go make a baby elsewhere."

"Kylayda Monroe, you will not sit here and talk about my brother like he is some fuckboy. Brodie loves you with everything in him, and he will never leave you. Now, as far as not having a baby, you need to get a couple more opinions before you just go off of what the first person told you. Now if you can't, then you can adopt. Stop crying baby, we will get through this. How long have you been holding this in?"

"I've known for a couple of weeks now, and it was killing me not to tell you, but I also didn't wanna talk about it. Bailey, I've been a complete mess. I've even been pushing my husband away. You know him, he ain't having that shit."

"You can't push him away, Ky. Shit, I'm sure this is hard for him as well. All that being insecure shit ain't cool, either. You don't wanna push him to another woman, now do you?"

"I know Bailey, I'm trying to do better, and of course not. I'll kill a bitch first and then make him call the clean-up crew. We in this until our caskets drop, and I mean that shit."

"You better mean that shit. Now go clean ya face and go home and do something nice for your man. Since you been treating him fucked up lately." Ky wiped her tears and smiled at me.

"Ok boss, I'm going, and don't get mad if I don't show up tomorrow."

"I'm not gone be mad. Go on home and relax. I love you, sis. And you can come to me for anything. It may be hard, but we gone work through this as a family."

"I love you too Bailey, and thanks for always being here for me."

"Ok bitch, enough of the mushy shit. Didn't I tell you to get out?"

I pulled Ky up, pulled her in for a hug, kissed her cheek, then pushed her out of the door. Once I was finished cleaning my desk off for the day, I rushed out of the office and headed home to hold and kiss all my babies. Hearing Ky tell me this had me a little sad, but I couldn't show her that. She needed me to be strong for her. My poor brother, I was gonna pay him a visit tomorrow to make sure he was good. The thing about Brodie was, he never acts like he's going through anything. He's always been my savior and everyone else's. Hopefully this time he'll let me be there for him because I know he at least needs a hug.

DEJA

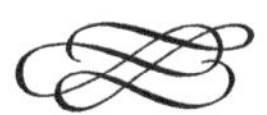

I was sitting in a bubble bath, soaking and listening to music, when I heard Jace come in the house screaming my name like a mad person. I didn't know what the hell was going on with him and I really didn't care. The bathroom door flew opened and this nigga had the look of anger on his face. The look that I know all so well.

"You didn't hear me fucking calling you, Deja?"

"No, Jace I didn't hear you. The music is on."

As soon as those words left my mouth, he grabbed me by my hair and pulled me out of the tub. I just knew I had bald spots in the middle of my head.

"You know what Deja, I'm starting to think you love getting ya ass beat. So, you met Miko yesterday?" Miko was the girl who's phone I called. Yeah they definitely had something going on he gave her a pet name in shit.

"I don't know who Miko is, Jace. Can you stop? You're hurting me."

"It's supposed to hurt, you stupid bitch. You thought it was cool to go through my phone?"

"No, Jace I'm sorry, I didn't mean to go through your phone."

He didn't say anything, but he did let my hair go once he threw me on the bed. I just laid there, curled up in a knot, scared as hell to move, because I didn't know what he was going to do next. Jace grabbed my leg and told me to turn over. Once I turned on my back I noticed he was ass naked. This nigga done came in the house and dragged me out of the tub just to fuck. If that's all he wanted, then he should have just asked. Now ain't nobody in the mood for this shit. But I wasn't gone say shit, I was gone lay there and let him do him. Hopefully he won't take too long to buss a nut. His dick was standing at attention, ready to enter me, but I wasn't wet or anything, and he didn't touch me or anything. He just rammed his dick inside of me.

"OUCH! Jace, you're hurting me."

My screams went unheard and he continued to drill in and out of me. After a while, my body started to react to him and I started to get wet. By then, I was in pain and I wanted him to stop. The weird part was he didn't say a word, he just kept pumping fast as hell. He's never done any shit like this before. I didn't know what set him off today, but I prayed once he came, he would fall asleep. A couple more quick pumps, and Jace was shooting his seeds inside of me. Once he finished he rolled on his side like he was ready to go to sleep. I went to turn on my side as well, and I guess he thought I was getting up.

"Deja, you better not move until I tell you to."

After he said that, he turned facing me, pulled me close to him, and wrapped his arms around me. My head was killing me, my pussy was sore, but the only thing I could do at this moment was stare out the window.

* * *

Waking up out of my sleep not able to scream or breathe, tears were running down my cheeks and Jace was on top of me, choking me.

"Let this be a little lesson, stay the fuck out of my phone. If you take it by mistake again, you might as well get ready to get ya ass beat."

I tried to say ok. I even tried to shake my head yes, but I couldn't. I felt like I was about to pass out. My eyes started to roll up inside my head, and that's when he let go. Once I finally caught my breath, he was still sitting there, staring at me like a killer. If he had kept choking me a little longer, I probably would be good and dead right now. After I caught my breath, I got up and walked to the bathroom in so much pain. I was still sore from last night, my head was still killing me. When I made it to the bathroom, I turned the water on and hopped in the shower. Here I was crying my eyes out, wondering when I was going to be strong enough to leave this nigga. How could I still stay after all the things he does to me? This can't be love at all. After I washed a couple of times then rinsed, I turned the water off, then stepped out. I dried off, then wrapped the towel around my body. When I made it in front of the mirror and took a look at my neck, all that was seen were Jace's handprints. I guess I wouldn't be going outside for anything for the next couple of days. There was a time when Jace wouldn't hit me anywhere where others could see. Now he's just getting reckless. The bathroom door opened, the Jace entered. He walked behind me and wrapped his arms around my waist, then kissed my cheek.

"Deja, you know I love you right?"

"Yes, and I love you too, Jace."

I didn't feel like saying it, but I also knew that could lead to another beating. To be honest with y'all, I do love Jace, but I don't know how much more of this I can take.

Jace

After losing Miko and getting put back down to trapping, I was pissed. Now I was standing in the mirror looking at what I did to my baby's neck, and now I was pissed. I didn't know how to control my anger and beating Deja did something to me. I know y'all think I'm sick and everything, but who gives a fuck. She still here, ain't she? If she didn't like what I do to her, she would leave.

"Go put some clothes on and relax, baby. When I'm done in the shower, I'll go out to get us something to eat." I kissed Deja's lips before she walked out of the bathroom. Once I made sure she wasn't standing in the hall, I closed the bathroom door and pulled my phone out. I've been trying to reach Miko and I guess she really wasn't fucking with me.

"I know you been seeing me calling you. Please baby, pick up. I don't want us to end like this."

After the message I left, I figured I would try again later. A half hour has passed and I was walking into the bedroom with a towel wrapped around my waist. Deja was sitting on the bed with her Kindle in her hand, so, I knew she was reading. L didn't bother her, I just let her do her and continued to get dressed. After I was completely dressed, I walked over to her kissed her forehead and told her I would be back. I was headed out to get us something to eat. Then I was gone chill with her all day since I didn't have to hit the streets until tonight, which was pissing me off.

Bro and Reem were gone get what was coming to them real soon. For now I was gone do this shit, but once I get my money up, I had a plan for they stupid asses. Once I jumped in my car, I pulled off, deciding to hit Publix up. Since I was trynna get on Deja's good side today, I figured I would cook her breakfast. It's been a minute since I've done some shit like this. Ten minutes went by, and I was pulling into Publix parking lot. After I parked the car, I jumped out and was heading to the store. I ran and grabbed some turkey bacon, eggs, cheese, pancake mix, orange juice, and some syrup. Once I had everything I needed, I made my way to the register.

"Mmmmmm, I wish I can come over for breakfast," this fine ass chick that was standing behind me cooed. This bitch was thirsty as hell. She was licking her lips and everything.

"Give me ya number and I might can make that happen for you," I advised her.

I handed her my phone and she punched her number in. When she handed me my phone back, I dialed her number so she would have mine.

"My name is Ivy, and yours?"

"Jace, baby girl and is that all you have?" She had a loaf of bread and some juice in her hand.

"Yes this is, I only needed a couple of things."

"Put it up there with my stuff, I got you." She did as she was told and we kicked it for a little more until the cashier was done ranging up my stuff. Once her stuff was rung up, I put it in a bag for her, then gave it to her.

"Thanks so much Jace, I really appreciate that, and I'll be looking forward to breakfast real soon."

"I got you Ma, I'll be calling you real soon."

She smiled at me then headed out the door. Baby girl had it going on. I watched as her hips swayed from side to side, as she walked out the door. Not only was she beautiful, but she had a bad ass a body to match. I had everything I needed, then I made my way back to my car. After twenty minutes, I was pulling back up to my crib and I saw my front door was open. As soon as I hurried and hopped out, an Uber was pulling up. I walked over to the window and he rolled it down.

"Here for Deja." The driver said.

"She good, my man."

He didn't ask any questions he peeled off with an attitude, and I didn't give a fuck. Once the car pulled off, I hit the lock buttons on my car and headed in the house. I stood by the door waiting for Deja to come back to the door. Soon as she came walking up, I was standing directly in front of her. Her eyes lit up like she just saw a ghost. I slammed the door shut, then grabbed her by her neck.

"So, where were you headed?"

"I was going to see my mama, Jace."

"Why the fuck are you lying, Deja? Since when you need bags to go see ya mama?" I said through gritted teeth right before I punched her right in her fucking eye.

"OUCH JACE!" Deja screamed as soon as my fist hit her face.

"Shut ya ass up, Deja. You're never leaving me and if you try again, I will kill you."

I was so fucking angry with her. If I had stayed out just a little longer, her ass would have left. Rage took over my mind and I threw her little ass on the floor and got on top of her, delivering punch after punch. Once I felt like she'd had enough, I got up and kicked her a couple of times. Looking at her bloody body laying on the floor I needed to get the fuck out of this house before I killed her ass today. I checked her pulse and she was still breathing, so I grabbed her face and turned it to mine.

"Get the fuck up and clean this blood up off my floor. Then take a shower, and get ya ass in the bed. I'm stepping out for a minute and if you're gone when I get back, I will hunt you the fuck down. Think I'm playing, and try me Deja."

After scaring her stupid ass, I knew she wasn't gone go anywhere, so I was out. I shot that shorty I'd just met in the store a text letting her know that she could have that cooked meal today if she wasn't busy. To my surprise she was all for it, so I started my car up and peeled off. When I made it back home, I had plans on changing all the locks on the door. I needed it to be locked so I can lock Deja's ass in the house. She thought this shit was a game for real, but I was dead serious. I would kill her before I let her leave me.

TAJI

"Hey baby, I'm so glad to see you," Monae screamed while jumping in my arms. I was at the airport picking her sexy ass up.

"I'm happy to see you too, Ma. So, are you ready to go meet my family?"

"Awwww baby, I thought we were gonna go get a hotel room."

"I never said that, Monae. What's wrong with us staying at my cousin's house?"

"Taj, we need our privacy, and they have little kids. You know kids annoy me."

Here she goes with her shit. What the hell did I get myself into? That's what the fuck I get for thinking with the head in my pants.

"We are staying at my cousin's house, and I ain't gone argue with ya ass. The house is so fucking big, we will be on one side of the crib, and they're on the other."

"Alright, damn baby, let's go. I'm tired from that flight and I need a nap," Monae cooed while kissing my cheek.

Once we made it to the car, I put her bags in the trunk and opened the passenger seat door for her. So, she could get in, I made sure she was in safe before I closed the door. I walked around to the driver's side, jumped in, then peeled off.

"Bailey was almost done with dinner when I left. So, it should be ready by the time we get there. I know you wanna eat before you lay down for your nap."

"I'm good Taji, you know I don't eat everybody's food."

I didn't say shit because it would probably start her smart ass mouth up. A half hour had passed and we were pulling in the driveway Monae's ass was knocked out. I guess she must be tired from the flight.

"Come on baby, we are here." When Monae opened her eyes and looked up at the house, her eyes lit up.

"Damn, this house big as hell. It looks bigger than ya dads house." I chuckled at her dramatic ass. This house was not bigger than my dad's, she was exaggerating.

"Girl, come on so you can meet my family."

I jumped out of the car and grabbed Monae's things out of the trunk. Then I walked around to help her out of the car. I walked up the steps with Monae following behind me. Once I opened the door, I let her go in first, then I walked in behind her.

"It's so beautiful in here and it smells good." I shook my head and kept on walking.

"Come on, let's go meet my cousin." We walked into the living room where I knew everyone was.

"Hey y'all, what's up. This is Monae."

"Hello, everyone." Monae spoke kind of dryly.

"Hey Monae, I'm Bailey, this is Reem, and our boys, Braylon and Braxton. Welcome to our home, and dinner will be available in about fifteen minutes. You can go ahead and freshen up."

"Thank you, so much."

"Alright y'all, let me show her our room and then we will be down. A nigga is starving."

"Ya ass always starving, Taji," Bailey said while smiling at me.

The smile was harmless, but I guess Monae didn't like it. Seeing the look on her face, I hurried and headed to my room without saying anything. I ain't never saw Bailey pop off and I wasn't trying to. Once we made it to my room, I opened the door and let Monae walk in first.

"I love this house, Taji. You didn't lie when you said we were way on the other side of the house."

"I told you the house is so fucking big we might never run into them unless we are going down for dinner."

"Well let me go clean up a little so we can go down to eat."

While waiting for Monae to come out of the bathroom, I leaned back on the bed and closed my eyes for a second. Once Monae made it in the room, I felt her little hands going into my pants. I knew we needed to get down to dinner, but my dick was standing at attention. Monae knew what she was doing and I wasn't mad at all. I needed to buss a nut. It's been a minute since I felt inside of her. After she stroked my mans a little longer, she was ready to climb on top of me, but I stopped her. I needed to grab a condom out of my drawer.

"Hold on Ma, let me get a condom."

"Why do you need a condom, Taji. It's not like I'm somebody new."

"Come on, Mo, don't ruin the moment, Ma. You already know how I get down. Why must we always have this discussion before sex? If I ain't using this condom, we ain't doing shit."

I didn't play about using protection. I didn't know what she was doing out in the streets and I wasn't ready to be nobody's daddy yet. My wife was gone be the mother of my kids and Monae wasn't her. She climbed off of me and let me get the condom. She saw how annoyed I was and she took it out of my hand, then pushed me on the bed. Once I was lying on my back she leaned over and took me into her mouth. The sucking, slurping, and gagging was turning me on. Monae was sucking my dick just like she missed a nigga.

"Mmmmm, I've missed you so much," she said in between sucks.

"Get up here and show me just how much you've missed me."

Monae put the condom on with her mouth, then she made her way on top of me and slid down on my dick. Her shit wasn't as tight as I would have liked it to be, which told me her ass been out here doing her. I ain't gone mention it. I was just gone enjoy this weekend and she didn't have to worry about me asking her ass to come back. Monae was all extra like I was blowing her back out. When I saw her eyes roll in the back of her head, I knew she was about to cum.

"Yesssssssssss Taji, yessssssss baby. Just like that. I'm about to cum, baby."

As soon as Monae announced she was about to cum, I sped up the pace, slamming in and out of her rough, just the way she liked. It also was turning me on. A couple more rough strokes, and I was shooting my seeds in the condom. After we were done, we both showered together and headed down for dinner.

"Sorry we're late. I dozed off while Monae showered."

"It's ok. We fed the kids first so we can all sit and eat together," Bailey said.

"So Monae, I hear you're in school. What's your major?" Reem asked.

"I'm undecided at the moment, but I do have my bachelors degree."

"That's what's up. Well, keep up the great work." While we were talking, Bailey was bringing our plates to the table. I thought Monae would ask if she needed any help, but her ass just sat there.

"Monae, why won't you go give B a hand." She sucked her teeth and rolled her eyes.

"I'm good Taji, thank you for looking out though," Bailey said, while rolling her eyes and walking back in the kitchen. I looked at Mo and gave her the side eye. I hated the way she acted sometimes. Something told me this visit was going to be long and annoying. Monae better not piss me off too much or I'd be shipping her ass back to Jersey earlier than Monday.

TYREEM

"I don't know about this little stuck up bougie ass little girl in my house, Reem."

"Calm down Ma, she's only here for the weekend."

"I know, but do you see her little stank ass attitude, and she got one more time to frown her face up at my kids."

"What you mean frowning up at the kids?"

"You already know how I am about mine. She even keeps looking at you when no one's looking. She better go on some damn where because I fight over the men in my life."

"Chill killer, you ain't doing shit to nobody. She's leaving Monday, and you probably won't see much of her while she's here."

"Taji deserves better. She's probably in the picture because of who he is and what he got. Stuck up gold digging ass bitch. She just doesn't know I'll beat her ass over Taji too, so she better not hurt his feelings." I sat and listened to Bailey go on and on about Monae. As soon as the dizzy chick walked in my crib, I knew Bailey wasn't gone like her. She walked in like she was better than everyone, and I peeped the way she was staring at me and licking her lips.

"When I get my cuz alone, I'll put him on game about her snake ass."

"So, you don't trust her either?"

"Nah, it's something funny about her ass, I just can't point my finger on it," Bailey chuckled, walked over to me, then straddled me.

"Look at us judging that girl and we just met her."

"I know right, that's crazy. But I wasn't feeling her actions when she first walked in the door."

"Enough about her. How is my baby doing? You've been extra busy this week for some reason."

"My fault baby, I lost one of my men on the day shift, plus Brodie been under a lot of pressure. So, I've been handling some extra work and getting the studio ready for Taji. After this week is over, I promise you'll have all my attention. What's wrong? Why are you looking so sad?"

"Ky told me what was wrong with them. I feel so bad for them."

"Yeah, me too. But they will get through this and we'll help them. They are two of the strongest people I know, not to mention how much they love each other."

"I know, but it's just so sad. They've wanted kids for so long."

"Baby I know, and it'll work out in their favor. You can't be stressing over it. Now tell me about your day."

"Well, we have a new client named Rayne, and she has a beautiful little girl named Eva. She's so young going through this shit it angers me, because she has a two-year-old daughter. When I was going through this the twins were not old enough to know. This baby is two, she sees what's going on."

"She good now, right? Y'all have her in your place?"

"Yeah, but I don't think she's ready. I mean, I hope she is. But I just don't know. Like, it took me almost to die to know I was done. Yeah, she just got out of the hospital, but she doesn't have anybody else in her life. Her mother disowned her. I had people who loved me and people who were I my corner. I think it's difficult to deal with when you're out here all alone."

Bailey loved her job and I was proud of what she did, but sometimes the shit was heartbreaking. I would rather her and Ky hire people to run the center and they work from home. Not because I want her home, but because I know this shit brings back up the years of abuse she went through. She claims talking about it and helping helps her cope with it better. So, whatever she wants, it's fine with me.

"Well baby, all you can do is pray for her. If this is what she wants, she will do any and everything to keep her and the baby safe."

"You're right, I'll pray about it and hope that we can help her."

"You and Ky are great at what y'all do. So I know she'll be fine," I assured Bailey while kissing her on her forehead.

"Thank you baby, you always know what to say. That's why I love you so much."

"I love you too, Ma. Yo, I can't believe I've loved you since I was fourteen." Bailey and I were now staring into each other's eyes.

"You really felt that strong for me at that age?"

"Yes. I mean, I had girlfriends growing up and I hit a couple of chicks here and there, but you were the only one I always wanted. When I moved back down here from Jersey, I planned to steal you from Leek's dumb ass," Bailey laughed.

"Reem, you crazy."

"I am crazy over ya fine ass, and I can't wait to make you Mrs. Price."

"Awwww, baby you really ready to get married?"

"Yup, I'm ready and it's definitely coming soon."

Bailey and I talk about marriage a lot, but I just hadn't popped the question yet. That's what I love about her the most is that she's not pushing the issue and she's waiting until I'm ready. My feelings for Bailey run deep, and I want nothing more than to spend the rest of my life with her. Which is why Brodie and I are going out to get her a ring tomorrow. My week is full of surprises for my family; Taji gets to see his studio he knows nothing about and I get to surprise my heart with an engagement dinner. Life is definitely going well for a nigga and I live for making my family happy.

"Are you ok, Reem?" Bailey asked taking me out of my thoughts.

"Of course I'm alright, look at this fine ass woman sitting on me, getting my dick all hard." I smiled at Bailey and she giggled like a little school girl.

"Mmmmm, I guess you want me to handle that for you?" I nodded my head yes, before pulling Bailey's lips to mine. We ended the night exploring each other's bodies.

BAILEY

Last night was everything, like always, with Reem. My baby knows how to make me feel good.

"What the hell you smiling at?" Ky asked walking into the office.

"Well damn bish, gm to you too, and if you must know, I was having flashbacks of how my man handled my ass last night."

"Ewww, I don't wanna hear that shit. Gm, mama so what's the day looking like."

"The usually chill day. We have no discharges or any new clients coming in," I assured Ky.

"That's good, because I'm fucking tired. My husband wouldn't let me sleep," Ky said while smiling.

"Don't start talking about ya night, you wouldn't let me talk about mine." We both burst out into laughter. My cell phone started to ring in my bag and I grabbed it to answer it.

"Hey Taji, what's up baby?"

"B, we need you. We have a client that's really fucked up, but we didn't wanna take her to the hospital. Can we bring her there?"

"Yes, bring her here and come to the back of the building, and text me when you arrive. Who is with you?"

"It's Samaad and me." I wanted to ask him where the hell that chick Monae was, but then I remembered the nanny was at the house. So, I would shoot her a text letting her know to keep an eye on that bitch.

"Alright, come on and bring her. Make sure y'all are not being followed."

"I got you. We on our way right now."

After I disconnected the call, I called the medical unit to have them get a bed ready for a new client. Once I was finished doing that, I hung the phone up so I could tell Ky what was going on.

"What happened?" Ky asked before I could say anything.

"That was Taji. He and Samaad have a possible client that's hurt. They didn't wanna chance taking her to the hospital so they wanted to bring her here."

"OH MY GOD! I hope she's ok. Do we have a doctor on staff today?"

"Yes, I believe Dr. Jones is in the building today. She's here doing check-ups today."

"Ok good, and you called medical. Let me go see if we have any available rooms for her."

Ky dialed the number to admissions to see if we had anything available, which I knew we would. The way we had this place running was unbelievable, but that was the advantage of purchasing your own building and having money to put whatever the hell you want in it. I know you all probably wondering how we keep it up. From us being a domestic violence center, we get plenty of donations, and a lot of support from different organizations. My phone was going off letting me know I had a text message. I opened it and it was Taj telling me they were pulling up in the back. I jumped up and headed out of the door with Ky following right behind me. Once we made it to the back door Taji had the girl in his arms. My heart broke instantly looking at her. Her lips were busted, both her eyes were black and swollen shut. After I got done staring in a daze, I jumped right into action.

"Come on, follow us this way," I told Taji, while Ky asked Samaad questions about the young lady. When we made it to the room, Dr. Jones was just walking in.

"Good Morning, Ms. Monroe. What do we have here?"

"A family friend was found in her home curled up on the floor. She did manage to crawl to her phone," Ky responded to the doctor. While the medical team took over, me, Ky, and the boys walked to my office. When we made it to my office, it was an awkward silence for a minute.

"Y'all can sit down if y'all want," I told the boys.

"How do y'all know her?" I asked.

"We grew up together in the projects. She's Jace girl."

"Jace that works for Reem?"

"Yeah man, I knew he was overprotective and would yoke her up at times, but I didn't know he was doing it like that." Samaad assured me.

"Wow, that's crazy I would have never thought. Does she have any family?"

"Her best friend is a close friend of mine, she already knows what happen. I told her I was taking her somewhere safe. As far as her mother, I don't think she should know she's here. She loves Jace and in her eyes, he does no wrong. So, she might not wanna believe he did this and we don't wanna take no chances of him finding her."

"I swear I wanna kill that motherfucker. I knew from day one something was off about his ass," Taji barked.

"Chill baby boy, you don't even know her like that to be killing someone. The thing about this situation is you have to let her wanna leave him. Killing him might make her hate you if leaving him wasn't what she wanted to do. Right now, just worry about getting her some help. Y'all did the right thing by bringing her here. Don't do anything to him, that could put her in a bad position. What we can do when she wakes up is see if she wants to press charges," I told Taji.

"Why do they stay, B? Someone hitting you is not love," Taji asked.

"When you're in a situation like this, you are screwed up mentally, and sometimes it takes years to understand that it was never your fault," Ky explained.

"I'm just so pissed the fuck off because Jace and I got into it the last time I went to his house. Deja came downstairs to get something to eat, and she had a handprint on her face. He and I had words and I let him know that if she ever came to me for help, I would help her. Not giving a fuck that he was my best friend," Samaad said.

"Samaad, it's not ya fault this happened, baby. To be honest with you, she wasn't ready to go. Because if she were, she would have told you when you were there."

The boys were fucked up over this and me and Ky had to calm them both down before they left out of here. We didn't want Jace's blood on their hands. Deja was safe here for the time being; once she was up and ready to talk, we would take it to the next step. Until then, I hoped they didn't kill that damn boy.

DEJA

Beep, Beep, Beep

I woke up out of my sleep with machines going off. I didn't know where I was, and the last thing I remembered was being strong enough to crawl to the living room to call Samaad. He was the only one that I knew would help me without him telling Jace. See, on a couple of different occasions, Maady told me he would help me if I ever needed help. I needed him at the moment. I knew I needed a hospital. I was in pain from the inside on out. Jace didn't even know if I was bleeding internally from the kicks he delivered. I guess he just didn't give a fuck about me.

"Hello I'm Ky, and I'm the founder and owner of this place. It's not a normal hospital, it's actually a domestic violence center. Now you're safe here and you can get the same medical attention as the hospital, but if you don't wanna be here, you can go as soon as you're able to," this lady said. I assumed she was Spanish the way her voice sounded. Of course, I couldn't see shit with my eyes swelled shut.

"Hello Ky, my name is Deja Simmons, and how did I get here?"

"Taji and Samaad brought you here. Samaad said once you called him, he knew something was wrong so he came to your rescue. They both are really hurting behind this."

I had to think for a second who Taji was. But then when I remembered, I thought to myself, *how the hell is he upset? He doesn't even know me.*

"Is Maady here?"

"No, he's not here. But if you want me to call him for you, I will."

"Yes please, can you ask him to find my best friend? I really miss her, and I hope she's not mad at me."

As soon as those words left my mouth, the tears started to fall. I was missing Tiombe like crazy, and I can't believe I let Jace keep me away from her. Ky got up and started to rub my back to soothe me.

"It's ok. I'll make sure I deliver the message. When the last time you saw anyone in your family?"

"It's been a while. Every time I talk to my mama, I tell her I'm busy with school and work so I don't have time. I always assure her that Jace and I would be to visit her soon. I guess because we talk on the phone often, she believes I'm ok. Plus, she loves Jace. She calls him her son-in-law and everything. When she sees us, she asks when we are gonna get married and give her some grandkids."

"How long have you and Jace been together?"

"For five years, I was eighteen and he was twenty. Jace was my world and he could do no wrong until the beatings started. Is it crazy that I love him even though he beats me?"

"No baby, you're not crazy. You just need help coping with all of this, and that's where we come into play. As long as you're here, we will keep you safe and help you move on with your life. Always know that there is life after this. I was once just like you. It took me to lose a life to know I had enough. So, as I told you earlier, as long as you wanna stay you are welcome. But if you wanna go, that's fine too. I'll call Samaad and tell him what you told me to, and I'll be back to sit with you until he comes, if you don't mind."

"I don't mind at all, Ms. Ky. I don't wanna be alone."

"Alright, give me a minute and I'll be right back."

Knowing that I was at a domestic violence center was so embarrassing. All the pain I was feeling, Jace really doing a number on me. Once he left yesterday morning, I found the Uber app on my phone and put the address in it to the closest hotel. Yeah, I had a card stashed away with a little money on it, so I was trynna hurry and leave. I didn't know how long he was gone be coming back, but I didn't think he would be back that soon.

"Ok, Samaad said he'd be here in a little bit and he will have your best friend with him," Ms. Ky said, bringing me out of my thoughts.

"Thank you for calling him for me."

"You're welcome. Now if you don't mind me asking, what triggered Jace off this time?"

"He came in the house and caught me packed up and ready to go. He beat my ass right in the front of the door, then grabbed his keys and left. But not before telling me to clean the blood up off the floor, then get a shower and get my ass in the bed."

"Trying to leave always angers them. Jace believes that you're so terrified of him that you will never leave. That's why he left you laying there like that. He just knew you were gonna be home when he gets back. Do you wanna go back or are you ready to get help and leave that life alone?"

"I love Jace, I really do, but I need to get out of this situation."

"Ok, well that's what I'm here for, to get you out of this situation. Inside, my center has everything you need, so you won't have to leave the building. We don't allow a lot of visits because we don't want to chance anyone following your family here. Not many people really know what this place is and we like to keep it this way."

"Ms. Ky, can I ask you something?"

"Yes you can ask me anything."

"When will I stop thinking about him?"

"Deja, this is all fresh to you, and Jace is all you know. It will take some time, baby girl. You just have to learn how to be strong. Jace will always be an unforgettable love. There was a time when y'all had good times, then there are those bad times that you'll never forget. It'll be hard to go on with life after this, but it will be all worth it. Knowing your worth and knowing it's more to life than being someone's punching bag is the best feeling ever. You'll get it together mama, trust me. It ain't easy, but I'll help as much as I can."

"OH MY GOD! Deja, what did he do to you?" Tiombe screamed, walking into the room with Samaad behind her. She ran over to me and kissed my cheek, and the minute we looked at each other, the tears started to run down both of our faces.

"I'm ok Tee, stop crying."

"Deja, you are not ok. Why didn't you tell me? I would have been helped you kill Jace," Tiombe fussed.

"I didn't want to get you involved."

"Deja I ain't trying to hear none of that, you already know how we do. I would have killed that motherfucker for you. You're my sister and you definitely didn't deserve this shit. Now I know why he was always so overprotective of you, and didn't want you to do anything. Why didn't I peep the signs. He's the reason you dropped out of school, isn't he?"

"Come on Tee, I don't wanna hear all of this. I've had a rough couple of days. I just want your company BFF, without all the judgment."

"Alright, my fault. I'm just pissed off, that's all. Hello I'm Tiombe, and you are?" Tee finally spoke to Ky after she chewed my ass out.

"I'm Ky, the owner of this place, and I'll also be Deja's mentor while she's here. You sound like my sister-in-law Bailey. That down for whatever friend," Ky said to Tee while laughing.

"Yup, that's me. I don't play about my BFF."

"Ok Deja, Imma leave you alone for your visit, and I'll be in my office if you need me. Just tell the nurse to call me," Ky said while walking out. Once she left I spent time with Tee and Samaad, telling them everything that happened to me. They just sat in listened without saying a word.

SAMAAD

When Ky called me and told me Deja was up and wanted me to see her and bring her BFF, I jumped up and threw some clothes on. Then, hit Tee up and told her I was on my way to pick her up. Once we made it to the center, Ky was in the room talking to Deja. I tried to hold on to Tee for a second so they could finish their conversation, but she wasn't having that. The time we'd been spending together, all she ever talks about is Deja. So I knew she couldn't wait until she saw her. We were now sitting and talking, and I couldn't believe that Jace had been doing all this to her for years. I wasn't here to judge though, so I just listened.

"So Maady, where did you find my BFF at?" Deja asked.

"Your BFF is about to be wifey as soon as she stops playing with a nigga's emotions."

"Boy, ain't nobody playing with ya emotions. I told you I'm ready," Tiombe said while smiling at me. She's right. We talked about it and she assured me that she was ready, but I ain't trynna get my feelings hurt.

"Wow, I never knew y'all two were checking for each other."

"Girl, Maady and I go way back. He was just one of my little secrets," Tiombe said while winking at me. I laughed then shook my head at her crazy ass.

"Hey y'all, what's good?" Taji asked.

"Yo bro, what are you doing here?"

"I came to see how Beautiful is doing?" He said while looking at Deja.

"Well hello, I'm Tiombe, Beautiful's BFF, and you are?"

"What's up Ma, I'm Taji. It's nice to meet you," Taji walked over to the bed.

"Hello Ms. Deja, how you feeling baby girl?"

"I'm ok Taji, thanks for asking." Deja said just above a whisper.

My boy has been checking for Deja since the first night he saw her at the club. He probably thinks no one peeped how he looked at her, but I did. I even peeped it the day we saw her at Walmart. Shit, when we picked her up from the house, he was tripping over it more than me. He was ready to kill Jace, and Bailey and I had to talk him out of it. We had been there for over an hour now and a nigga was kind of tired. So we said our goodbyes, promising Deja that we would see her tomorrow. I kissed her forehead and Tee kissed her cheek. Then I dapped Taj up and we headed out of the door. Once we made it to the hall of the center, Tiombe just broke down crying. I grabbed her, then pulled her in for a hug.

"What's wrong baby? Why are you crying?"

"I feel so bad that I didn't know the signs, Maady. Why wasn't I there to help my BFF? Do you see her face? That motherfucker needs his ass beat the fuck up."

"He will get his baby, just calm down. It's not your fault and you can't beat ya self up about it. The best thing for you to do is be here for her while she's going through this hard time. Now stop crying, and come on so I can get you home."

Tee wiped her face and grabbed my hand, then we walked out the center, holding hands. When we made it to the car, I opened her door for her, and made sure she was in safe. Then I walked around to the driver's side and hopped in.

"Samaad, can I stay with you tonight? I just don't wanna be alone."

"You already know you never have to ask that, Tee. You're always welcome at my home, baby girl. Do you need to stop by your crib to get some stuff?"

"Yes, we can go to my house since it's on the way."

"Oh yeah, Ky and Bailey don't want anyone to know where Deja is. Their center is kind of off the radar. Not many people know it sits back there. Hell, people don't even know what it is. When I first walked in it, I was so amazed at what they did."

"They don't have to worry about me saying a word, and yes that place is nice. Who's it named after?"

"Lexi was Ky's daughter that she was pregnant with years ago. She was in an abusive relationship and her baby's father beat her up at nine months, which caused her to go into labor. He left her in the house to die and because of the baby not making it to the hospital, and Ky delivering her while she was out cold, the baby didn't make it. So, Ky owns the center and Bailey does most of the hands-on work. They make an awesome team."

"Wow, that's sad. But they are doing this for a good cause. Was Bailey in an abusive relationship too?"

"Yes, her situation was kind of like Deja's. She was beaten badly and left in the house to die. "

"They have to be strong people to be able to help a whole center full of ladies when they still battle with this shit themselves. I know they probably still have nightmares. I wonder if they can keep men after some shit like this."

"Well Ky is married and Bailey is soon to be engaged to Reem. Reem is the one who found her in the home all beat the fuck up. They have great relationships. I asked them how do they stay straight in their relationships, and they told me that it's life after abuse. They also said it takes a strong man to love a broken woman."

"Wait, Reem is the dude you work for? Him and that dude Bro, right?"

"Yeah, Bro is Ky's husband."

"Oh ok, well I hope Deja is done with Jace this time. You know how some girls keep going back."

"Yeah, I know. Me, too. I don't ever wanna see her in a situation like this ever again."

"I'll pray for her, and make sure to be by her side while she's trying to get her life back on track."

"When you wanna go back up there let me know and I'll take you."

"Samaad, I do have my own car. I can drive myself."

"Ok, my fault. Well drive ya self then," I said while smiling at her.

"I didn't mean it like that. I'm just saying I know you be having shit to do. Sometimes we can go together, but other times I know you may have something to do."

"I knew what you meant, beautiful, and that's fine."

Tee smiled at me then started looking out the window. I didn't know what her and I were about to get into, but I was happy to be spending time with her.

TAJI

Getting out the house to see Deja was hard as hell with Monae at the crib. I had to lie to her and tell her I had to make a run for Reem. She cussed and fussed not wanting me to leave, but she eventually gave in and took her annoying ass to sleep. Now I was at the center and Samaad and Tee had just left. I was sitting next to Deja's bed just staring at her. The way her face looked angered me, but I knew she wouldn't wanna talk about what happened to her. So I just sat quietly, waiting for her to say something.

"Can I ask you a question?" Deja asked.

"You can ask me anything you want, Beautiful."

"Why are you here? Like, you barely know me and I hear that you carried me in here and now you're checking on me. Like, you know nothing about me, but you here."

"I ain't gone lie, baby girl. I've been thinking about you since the first night in the club. I'm not no stalker or anything, because I wasn't looking for you, I just knew I was gone see you again. That day I saw you in Walmart, I just knew something was meant to be. Even if we just become friends, I'll be cool," I said while laughing.

"Taji, why would you even wanna be my friend? I have a lot going on in my life right now, and I wouldn't wanna bring no one else in my drama."

"Don't do that, baby girl. You need some people to be close to you right now to help you get through all of this. Now I'm not here to judge you at all, and I don't care to talk about what happened to you. If you want to talk about it, I will listen. But if you don't talk about it, I won't ask. What I do know is there is something about you that makes me want to get to know you. If you want me to go, I'll go. But I ain't gone promise you I'm not coming back," I assured her.

"So, you just gone just make me be your friend?" Deja said while smiling.

"There goes that beautiful smile. I knew I could get one before I leave."

"You about to leave?"

"I was, but if you don't want me to, I'll stay a little bit longer."

"Can you stay a little longer? I don't think I'm gone get much sleep tonight."

Since she didn't want me to go, I pulled a chair up and sat next to her bed.

"So, Ms. Deja tell me about ya self, Ma."

"Well, I was born and raised here in Atlanta. I'm an only child. I graduated school top of my class. I was a student at Clark-Atlanta until Jace stopped me from going to school. Tiombe and I have been best friends from birth. Our mothers are also best friends. I'm unsure of what I wanna do with my life now that I'm trynna start over, but I would love to own some type of business." When she got done telling me all that, I noticed the sadness in her voice.

"What's wrong Ma, you started out good, then you got sad all of a sudden?"

"Just thinking that I'm twenty-three years old and don't have shit going for myself. This shit is crazy. Never in a million years would I have thought my life would be so fucked up right now."

"Calm down Ma, it's not like you can't change. While you're here, use your time wisely. Start your classes back up online than work it out from there."

"Enough about me, Taji. Tell me something about you, Mr. Jersey."

"Oh, so I see you remember where I'm from."

"Yup, and Reem is your cousin."

"Oh ok. So you were paying attention at the club, I see. My name is Taji Price and I'm twenty-three. I'm from Camden which is a little city in New Jersey. I'm down here to get my music business on and popping, and I also wanted a different atmosphere."

"Can you sing, or you just looking to produce?" I looked at her then smiled. I figured instead of answering her question, I'd just sing a couple of verses to something. The lyrics to Tank's song *So I Can Have You Back* popped in my head, so I started to sing.

I hope he makes the biggest mistake

The unforgivable that makes your heart break

I hope you tell him 'sorry is just not enough'

Before I finished the last little bit of the verse, Deja was clapping her hands and cheering me on.

"Wow Taji, your voice is amazing. How long have you been singing?"

"Thanks Ma, and I've been singing since I was little, like five. Of course all the dudes in my family are into the streets, so that's what my dad expects me to do. He wants me to take over his empire, and that's not what I wanna do. Music is my life and I'm gonna follow my dreams, regardless if he likes it or not."

"Oh ok, well you have a new fan, and I wish you all the luck in the world. Do you wanna sing or own your own label?"

"I really wanna own a label and produce, but I'll sing from time to time. So, I'll definitely be doing an album after I get a studio and a couple of clients."

"That's what's up. You have it all mapped out."

My phone started going off in the middle of our conversation. I looked at it, saw it was Monae, and I hit the ignore button. I didn't feel like arguing with her, so I turned my phone off. Once I slid my phone into my pocket, Deja and I continued to talk about all types of stuff. I knew it was late and I didn't belong in here, but I shot Bailey a text letting her know I was here, in case someone gave her or Ky a call.

JACE

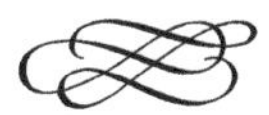

It's been a couple of days since I been home. After I kicked Deja's ass I went and spent some time with Ivy. Baby girl got some good ass pussy, had me over her crib stuck for two days. Shit, I hadn't even been out on the streets so I knew Reem and Bro were gone be looking for my ass soon. Once I told Ivy I would be back later, I headed to my house. After about twenty minutes, I was pulling up in my driveway. I turned the car off, then jumped out, and made my way up to the door to go in the house. Once I entered the house, it was blood still on my fucking floor, which angered me instantly.

"DEJA!" I yelled while heading up to the room to see if she was still sleeping.

When I made it upstairs and I didn't see her ass, I was furious. I pulled my phone out of my pocket and dialed her number, but to my surprise, the number said it was no longer in service. This fucking bitch done grew balls and left me. She better hope I don't find her ass. Grabbing a duffle bag and throwing some shit in it, I figured I'd better get out of here in case the cops come. Deja done fucked everything up. Now Imma have to lay low. *Fuck, laying low means I can't even make no money,* I thought to myself. If I find that little bitch, I swear she's as good as dead. Pulling my phone out once again, I figured I'd call her mom to see if she's heard from her. I dialed her number and she picked up on the first ring.

"Hey my baby, how you been?"

"Hey mom, have you saw Deja?

"Jace, what you mean have I saw Deja?"

"Mom, I've been out of town for a couple of days and she's not here."

"Well I haven't talked to her. Maybe she's with Tiombe."

"Do you know her address?"

"I'll text it to you once I hang up, and keep me posted Jace. Let me know as soon as you find Deja."

"Alright mom, I sure will."

I don't know why Deja's mom loves me so much. If she had any sense, she would wanna know why I didn't already know Tiombe's address if her and Deja are best friends. My phone vibrated and I knew it was the address from Deja's mom. Once I finished getting my clothes and the money out of my safe, I was headed out the door, and my first stop was Tiombe's house. Tiombe's house was about a half hour away and I was pissed because it was out of my way. Once I got there, her car was parked out front, so I was kind of glad she was here.

I jumped out of my car and banged on the door a couple of times. One of her neighbors came out of their home and told me they saw her leave last night. Nosey ass old lady is telling her business. I didn't even respond, I just jumped in my car and headed to Ivy's house, hoping she was still home. I was speeding down the Atlanta streets, in my feelings, wondering where the fuck Deja took her ass. She shocked the hell out of me. I never thought her ass was gone leave. I was pulling up to Ivy's crib. I sat for a minute trying to get my mind together, I knew how I was when I was angry and I didn't wanna show Ivy that side of me. Once I felt like I was ok, I got out of the car and knocked on her door.

"You back so soon."

"Yeah, I had a change in my plans today. Were you about to leave or something?"

"No, I was chilling. I told you I'm on vacation from work this week."

"Oh ok, so can a nigga keep you company again today?"

"Sure, come on in."

When I walked in it smelled like she was cooking something and my stomach started growling.

"What you in here cooking?"

"Hooking some lunch up. Why, you hungry?"

"Yeah, I can eat."

I followed her to the kitchen, sat at the table, and watched her switch around the kitchen doing her thing.

"You eat grilled chicken caesar wraps?"

"Yeah, is that what you are making?"

"Yes, with some french fries, and I guess I'm on the menu for dessert," Ivy said while winking at me. I smiled and shook my head at her freaky ass.

"I think I'll like that. Can I ask you something, sexy?"

"You can ask me anything you want."

"Why are you single?"

"I'm not ready to commit to anyone, that's why I'm single."

Her saying that caught me off-guard. Now I wanted to know did she have a lot of friends.

"So, you have other friends like me?"

"I have friends Jace, but I ain't fucking all of them if that's what your question is."

"You not fucking all of them, but you fucking some of them?"

"I'm fucking one of them and I'm grown as hell with no man, so I can fuck whoever I want. Do you have a problem with that? I hope not, because I know you have a damn girl somewhere."

"Nah you good, Ivy. I was just asking, Ma."

Ivy was straight to the point and wasn't afraid to say what was on her mind. I don't know how Imma deal with her ass, but she could be something to do until I get my bitch back home.

TYREEM

"Yo Bro, did you hear about that shit with Jace?"

"Yeah, Ky told me about it. As soon as she told me I thought back to the night when he dragged baby girl by her arm out of the club."

"I was thinking the same thing, and I think that's why he doesn't like Taji. He probably feels like he's a threat. I saw shorty staring at him, so I know he saw her little ass starting too."

"Had my wife come home late as hell the other night. She's getting attached to that girl already."

"She ain't the only one getting attached to her. Man, Taji stayed out all night sitting next to that girl's bed. While Monae bougie ass was at my crib in his bed."

"Yo, lil homie was wrong for doing that," Brodie said while laughing.

"He reminds me of how I was with Bailey while she was recovering."

"Tell him to be careful. He doesn't know if baby girl gone wake up one day and want her man back."

"I know right, shit Samaad and Bailey said they had to talk him out of going to go kill Jace's ass."

"Say word, that shit is crazy as fuck. We know exactly how he feels, though."

"What's up with Jace, though. He hasn't even been to work, and I doubt if he will show up. His punk ass is probably scared that the cops are looking for his ass. Remember how Leek did. That nigga went to the next town, scared as hell. Pussy got that nigga caught up, though."

"Ain't nobody looking for Jace, though. Bailey said they gone talk to baby girl today about pressing charges."

"Well, that nigga will show up soon as he runs out of money. He ain't making shit if he is not working."

"That's true," I said while laughing.

"So, since Bailey been so busy, you haven't been able to set her engagement dinner up. Now what were you gone do?"

"Man, Imma go to her job with flowers in shit and just pop the question. I ain't got time to be trynna keep up with this crazy schedule her ass be doing. I wish her and Ky would just hire somebody to run the place so they can stay home and enjoy life."

"Now you know that ain't even happening, so get it out of your head. I tried that shit one time, and Ky and me got into a big fight over it. She told me I was trynna run her life, and she didn't talk to me for days. I left that conversation alone and I'm never bringing it up. If she love her job, I love it too. Happy wife, happy life and that shit is the truth," Brodie said looking so serious. I couldn't do anything but laugh at his ass.

"Since Jace haven't shown up lately, did you put anybody on his corner?"

"Yeah, I put Quan's little brother on it. He came to me telling me that he hadn't seen Jace, and if we didn't have anybody on that corner that his brother can handle it."

"Alright cool, thanks for handling that for me. I've been so fucking busy I haven't been able to do shit."

"You know I got you, Reem. What you about to do now?"

"I'm waiting for Taji to come so I can take him to the studio. But then I think I should wait until he takes that hood booga to the airport."

"Why you don't like that girl? You done called her about three different names since we've been talking."

"I don't know. It's just something about her, and I already told Taji how I felt. Shit, ya sister peeped it to."

"Oh shit, Bailey likes everyone. If she doesn't like somebody, yeah something is up with that person."

"Taji don't really like her ass anyway." We both fell out laughing.

"What y'all in here laughing about," Taji asked walking into our office.

"You, little nigga. What you up to today?" Bro asked.

"Nothing. Reem asked me to stop here. What's up, cousin?"

"I wanted you to go on a run with me. Where bad and bougie at?"

"She's in the car. I tried to get her to stay in the house but she wouldn't."

"Man, why you ask that girl to come down here if you gone keep leaving her in the house?" Brodie asked.

"She doesn't wanna do shit but stay in the house and fuck. I'm good on her ass, I'm ready for her to go back home. She's been so annoying since she's been down here. Everything is an argument when we are not doing what she wanna do."

"Well, maybe that's why she came. She misses the dick, little cuz."

"She should have kept it tight while she was home. Then maybe it would be enjoyable enough to stay in all day every day." Brodie and I both burst out laughing.

"Wait what, you got a loosey-goosey at the house?" We all began laughing even harder.

"Shut the hell up Reem, you stupid as hell," Taji said.

"Well I hope if you hit you used protection since she is giving up the goods. Damn man, you haven't even been here long and she couldn't wait."

"That's what I'm saying. Boys from back home always would warn me about her, but I just thought they were hating. She is like a big deal back home, so I thought they were just jealous and wanted her for themselves. When in all reality, she was probably giving them the goods. These hoes ain't loyal."

"Speak for ya self my nigga. My wife is very loyal."

"Shit, my girl is loyal, too," I said.

"How did y'all know that y'all girls were the ones. How did you know they didn't just want what you had."

"For me, Kylayda was always about making her own money. She's always had some type of job. She also is a daddy's girl. He still will give her anything she wants. My wife was doing damn good before she met me. So, I knew it wasn't my money. I knew she was the one for me when she hung around before we made it official. When I realized I wasn't getting any younger, I figure I'd better hurry up and wife her before another nigga does," Brodie explained.

"As for me, Bailey grew up in money. Her brother took care of her from day one. We've been best friends forever, so I knew she was all I wanted in life. I also knew I had some big shoes to fill because Brodie had made her a little-spoiled princess. Once I knew she was all I wanted, I made a move on her." I assured Taji.

"Is it hard dealing with a damaged woman that went through what they've gone through?"

"Absolutely, but it's all worth it when you have the love of your life. You just have to be strong enough for the both of y'all on those days she's not strong. What are all these questions about, cuz?"

"Oh nothing, I was just wondering."

"Yeah, ok youngin. This is about ole girl ain't it?" Brodie asked.

"I guess you could say that. I don't know what it is about her, but ever since I first saw her, I've wanted to get to know her. Have y'all ever just looked at someone and wanted to know everything about them?"

"Nah, not me. I already told you I've always wanted Bailey since we were young as hell. So, any other chick I dealt with wasn't anything more than a piece of ass or something to do until Bailey was ready. What about you, Brodie?"

"Yeah, I knew from the day I first saw Ky that she was gonna be mine. Of course, her little ass made me chase her before she finally gave in. But listen youngin, we know you are feeling ole girl. It's not easy though, when loving a woman that is damaged, and you just met her, too. You have to make sure she's done with Jace before you put all your feelings into her. She might think she's done with him, but she might not be. Granted that she needs to be done, but sometimes these women are so messed up over these dudes. That's why they need help. But you can't help them if they not ready. Just protect your heart youngin, that's all I'm saying."

"I got you, but it's definitely a struggle. Like, how the hell do I feel like this already and I just met baby girl?"

"I don't know little cuz, but just be careful, that's all. Now, come on and take a ride with me. As a matter of fact, I'm getting in ya car and tell you where to go. If we get in my car, I might have to put ya bitch out if she starts her shit."

"Nah she was gone be on her best behavior because she like you," Taji said laughing like that shit was cool. I didn't find that shit funny at all, but apparently he didn't give a fuck.

"Like, how could you just laugh about that shit?" I asked.

"I don't care who she likes. Her ass could go on back home and fuck whoever she wants. I don't care once she leaves, I'm changing my number. It's no need for her to keep in touch with me anymore. She fucking whoever she wants anyway."

Once I grabbed my phone and keys, I left out and told Bro I'd be back soon.

BAILEY

"Hello Rayne, how are you? I was coming to check on you and to let you know that you're gonna be getting a roommate today. Is that ok with you?"

"I don't mind, as long as they don't mind me having a kid."

"She's fine with that. We already explained everything to her and as soon as we have an available room, we will separate you two."

"Ms. Monroe, I actually don't mind the company. I get real lonely in here sometimes."

"Alright, well she'll be in shortly, and I'm going to go handle some business. If you need anything just come to my office."

After I got done letting Rayne know about her roommate, I headed back to my office. Walking in my office, it was full of flowers. I mean they were everywhere.

"Damn, you must have put it on my bro last night," Ky said while laughing.

"Girl, I don't know what has gotten into him lately. He's been talking about marriage heavy the past couple of weeks. I think he's about to pop the question Ky, I just don't know when."

"Well, are you ready sis?"

"Yes, I am so ready to be Mrs. Price. Let me call my man and thank him for all these beautiful flowers." I pulled out my phone and dialed his number, and he picked up on the first ring just like I knew he would.

"What's up, beautiful."

"Hey baby, I was just calling you to thank you for all these flowers. What did I do to deserve all of these?"

"You know what you did last night," Reem said while laughing.

"Really Tyreem!"

"Sike, Ma I'm only joking. You know you deserve the world, and I just wanted to show you how much I love you today."

"Awwwww, baby that's so sweet. You know you mean the world to the boys and me. We love you so much, and I can't wait to spend the rest of my life with you."

After Reem and I got done talking nasty for a little bit, I assured him that it was on in popping when I got home today. I've been working like crazy lately so we haven't really been spending much time together. Tonight, I was gone go home and tend to my man.

"Are you ready to show Deja her new room?" Ky asked, bringing me out of my thoughts.

"Oh shit, my fault sis. I was just in another world."

"That's that love shit. Reem got ya ass on cloud nine right now. I get it though, that's the best love ever when it's been years and that nigga still make you get butterflies in your stomach."

"Right, I'm enjoying life with my man and kids. Three years ago, I would have never thought I would have made it this far. I just knew Leek was gone kill my ass."

"Yeah I felt the same about Donte, but look at us now, stronger than ever. Now come on so we can introduce Deja to Rayne."

Ky jumped up and headed out the office and I followed right behind. We were on our way to the medical wing of our building. It took us about five minutes to get there and once we walked in, Deja was sitting on the side of the bed.

"Hey mama, how are you feeling?" Ky asked.

"Hello Ms. Ky and Ms. B, I'm feeling ok. I can't wait to meet my roommate, I need someone my age to talk to."

"Well she's ready to meet you as well. Now remember, she has a two-year-old, and this is only a temporary stay. Until we have an open room to move you in," I assured Deja. I helped her up and we all headed to her room. Once we made it to the room, the door was already opened and Rayne was on the bed reading a book.

"Hey Rayne, this is Deja, and Deja, this is Rayne." They both spoke and then we left to let them get more acquainted.

"So what's next on the schedule today?" I asked Ky.

"We can plan our anniversary fun day if you want to."

"Yeah that's cool. Let's get that out of the way before we get swamped with work again."

"Let's go to the conference room real quick. I need to pick something up."

As soon as we walked into the room and Ky turned the lights on, I was in shock. The conference room was set up like a dinner party was about to go down. Taji was standing in the corner. The minute I walked in, he started singing one of my favorite songs. *Why I Love You* by Major.

I found love in you, and I've learned to love me too

Never have I felt that I could be all that you see

It's like our hearts have intertwined and to the perfect harmony

This is why I love

I couldn't believe they all set this up, and Ky's slick ass knew all about it. When Taji got done singing the chorus part, Tyreem got on one knee in front of me.

"Baby, since I can never get you home because you are always here working late, I figure I would come to you. Bailey Monroe, I've wanted you to be my wife ever since we were fourteen years old. I knew we were young, but I've always known you were the one for me. Even when I moved away, we still were the best of friends, keeping in touch. When I moved back and saw you had a man, my heart was crushed, but that didn't stop us from being best friends. Bailey, I'm sick of just being your man. Baby I wanna be your soulmate, husband, and the one you grow old with. Bailey, will you marry me?"

The tears were rolling down my face. I knew he was going to ask me to marry him, but to actually witness all of this, I was the happiest woman in the world.

"Yessssssss baby! Yessss baby, I will marry you."

After Reem put this big ass rock on my finger, I pulled him up off the floor, and pulled him in for a hug and a kiss.

"I love you baby, and you can have the wedding of your dreams."

"Alright Reem, move out my way and let me hug my sister," Ky said while pushing Reem out of the way.

"Ya slick ass knew all about this, didn't you?"

"Yup, and I'm so happy for you mama." Ky said while kissing my cheek. After Ky and I got done hugging, then my brother walked over and pulled me in for a hug.

"Congratulations baby girl, I'm so happy for you. Reem has always been good to you and my nephews and I wish you guys nothing but the best," Brodie said.

"Awwww, Bro, thank you. I love you more," I assured my brother while kissing his cheek. I couldn't forget about Taji, his little ass sang the shit out of that song.

"Taji, thank you baby for singing my favorite song. Boy, ya voice is every bit of amazing. I can't wait until you put it to use."

"Thank you Bailey and you're welcome, and I'll be singing at the wedding, I hope."

"Of course you will be, cuz. Why would you ask that?"

Ky and I set the food up and we all sat and ate lunch together. Today was a great day and after work, I was going home with my fiancé."

DEJA

I was now in my new room lying across the bed in my own thoughts. It's been a couple of days since I saw Jace. I didn't know why I was thinking about him after he did what he did to me.

"You miss him, don't you?" Rayne asked. At first I felt like I was gonna get an attitude, but I kept it cordial since we both were here for the same reason.

"I don't know if I miss him or if I'm worried about how he's doing. Hell, I was just scared he might find my ass. My head so messed up right now I don't know whether I'm coming or going."

"Girl, I miss my daughter's father, so much. Am I crazy for missing him?"

"If you are crazy then I'm crazy, too. We shouldn't be worried about these niggas. They hurt us," I chuckled because I knew that shit was easier said than done.

"Do you believe what Ms. B says when she says there is life after abuse? Like, will somebody be able to love us? Will we be able to love someone without being scared of them? I'm thinking about starting those counseling sessions. I really do need them. I'm having nightmares like crazy, and Eva asking for her father is not helping at all."

"I don't know much about you Rayne, but I know we are here for the same situation. How about while we are here, we help each other get through this?"

"That sounds like a plan. We can motivate each other to get our new lives up and running. Do you have any kids?" Rayne asked.

"No, I don't have any kids. How is it taking care of little mama? Is it hard?"

"It definitely is, but I wouldn't change it for anything in the world. She is my everything."

"That's what's up. Do you have any family?"

"My mother disowned me when I dropped out of school. Terrell felt like I didn't need to go to school, I just needed to be home and take care of Eva."

"My mom is around, but she thinks Jace does no wrong."

"Does she know he beats on you?"

"No, nobody knew. He kept me in the house away from the world. He made me stop going to school. I couldn't even chill with my best friend. I couldn't do shit, but cook, clean, and do whatever Jace wanted. He didn't even want me to read my Kindle. Whenever I was all into a book and I didn't hear him when he called me, that was a slap right upside the head. Then he would take my Kindle for days."

"Oh wow, that sound like some stupid shit Terrell would do. So, you like to read? I do too, what's the last thing you read?"

"*I need you bad* by Chanique J. Girl, I love Shan Presents authors, they always keep them bangers coming."

"Right girl, I love Shan Presents too. I was thinking about writing a book," Rayne said.

"Shit, we both can write a damn book the shit we been through. Why don't you go ahead and write one?"

"Terrell wouldn't let me do it before, but I think I just might do it now."

"You really should shit, we both can do one. I'll start tonight, and we both can figure out how to get them published when we are finished."

"Great, that sounds like a deal," Rayne agreed. There was a knock at our door and Rayne jumped up to answer it.

"Hey, is Deja in here?" I heard Taji's voice. I jumped up and fixed my hair with my hands. Then I looked down at my clothes to make sure I didn't look too bad.

"Hold on a minute, let me make sure she's up to seeing you."

"Alright, tell her it's Taji."

"Ok, I will, Mr. Taji," Rayne said right before she shut the door.

"Oh my God! I look a mess. What is he doing here?"

"I don't know, but apparently he wants to see you. Here, put this on and let me brush your hair a little." Rayne gave me a cleaner looking shirt to put on and she fixed my hair. I still had the bruises on my face, but the swelling went down a little.

"I think he likes me, but why can't he see I'm no good for him."

"Don't say that, Deja! Ms. Ky always says there is life after what we've been through. Besides, how you know he just not trynna be a friend."

"I guess you're right. Open the door, before he leaves." Rayne opened the door and I walked over and was standing face to face with Taji.

"What's up, Beautiful?"

"Hey Taji, what's brings you up here?"

"My cousin had a surprise lunch for B, he just proposed to her. She told me to come get you two."

Rayne grabbed Eva and we all headed to where the party was. Once we made it to the room, we all walked in together and everyone spoke. The two dudes I remembered from the club were here. An awkward feeling came over me and I think it was because of the bruises on my face. I was ready to turn around and walk back out the door, but Taji grabbed my hand.

"It's cool Ma, you're still the most beautiful girl in the room," he said while whispering in my ear.

When he said that in my ear, he made me feel a little better. I walked over to Bailey and congratulated her, and she showed me her ring. We all mingled and talked amongst each other. Eva had her a good old time she was stuck to Ms. Ky's husband. I guess he reminded her of somebody.

"Eva get over here," Rayne fussed.

"She's good over here with us, and by the way my name is Brodie. I'm Ky's husband."

"Hello, Brodie my name is Rayne and that little one that's bothering you is Eva."

"She's beautiful Rayne, and she's not bothering us. How old is she?"

"She's two going on twenty-two," Rayne said and everyone laughed.

Rayne and I continued to enjoy our afternoon with Ms. B and Ms. Ky. I guess being here getting my life back on track wouldn't be bad after all.

JACE

"Alright Jace, it's been over a week and ya ass still in the same damn spot," Ivy fussed.

"Come on Ma, leave me alone. I ain't bothering you."

"Look nigga, it was fun, but ya time is up. I don't know what happen to you and ya girl, but I'm not the one. We ain't in no type of relationship, and you are blocking my other friends from coming around. I don't know what that bitch did to you or what you did to her, but you better go on home and fix it. You can't stay here. I already told you what it was."

Hearing her call Deja a bitch angered me worse than what I already was. I jumped up and grabbed her by her neck, then lifted her up off her feet.

"You better watch ya mouth when you are talking to me, Ivy. I don't do disrespect. Do you understand me?" I barked.

She couldn't speak because of how tight I was holding her neck, but she managed to nod her head yes. Once she did that, I dropped her little ass, and she fell to the floor all out of breath. While she was lying on the floor getting herself together, I put my shoes on, grabbed my keys, and walked out of the door. These bitches were getting beside themselves lately. I made it out of the door and hopped in my car, but before I pulled off, Ivy was running out of the house with my bag in her hand.

"Here you go, bitch ass nigga. Take ya shit and don't come the fuck back here."

After she threw my shit on the ground, she ran in the house and locked her door. I didn't go after her. I figured fuck her, it was time for me to leave her house. I missed Deja so bad and I was running out of funds. It was time to make some shit shake before my ass ended up homeless with no food. I knew I could always go to my mom's house, even though I didn't fuck with her like that. My phone ringing was taking me out of my thoughts.

"Yo, my nigga, what's good? Why haven't you been out on the block?" Quan asked.

"Man, I got caught up in some shit. But check this, I need to borrow a couple of bands. Do you think you can look me out?"

"Come on now Jace, you know I ain't got it like that. Ya ass needs to be out here putting in work."

I wasn't trying to hear this shit. All I wanted was the money, and since he wouldn't give it to me, I would just rob his ass tonight.

"Quan, I ain't trying to hear all that. If you don't have it just tell me you don't have it."

"Nigga, don't be fucking talking to me like you got a problem, man later," Quan barked.

Before I heard a dial tone. *Did this nigga just bang in my damn ear,* I said to myself while looking at my phone. At this point, I didn't have a clue what to do with myself. I still didn't know where Deja ass was, and still hadn't caught up with Tiombe's hoe ass. Then I remembered she still attended Clark Atlanta, so I decided to head to her school and see if I caught up with her. After twenty minutes, I was now pulling up to the campus. I happened to remember where she parked at because that's where I used to meet Deja when I used to pick her up from school. I looked around the parking lot and didn't see her car, but I still decided to sit and wait for a little bit to see if she was riding with someone else. While I was waiting, I saw a car pull up that looked like Samaad's car. As soon as he pulled up to the door, Tiombe came walking out. What the fuck were these two doing together? I didn't want them to see me, so I waited until they pulled off before I pulled out behind them. I was sure that following them they would lead me right to Deja.

* * *

Hours had gone by and I was still following these two around, and they hadn't lead me to Deja yet. Now we were pulling up to Tiombe's house and they were standing on the step, kissing each other. Then they went inside. I waited a couple more minutes and when I saw he wasn't coming back out, I decided to leave. Maybe they'll lead me to her another time. Samaad's ass done moved up. He got the fucking job that I should have and he got a bitch. Must be nice. This nigga living the life and here I am all fucked up in the game.

Angry and annoyed, I was ready to go rob one of these corner boys, since my money was running low. I knew at this time that Quan was probably on his way in the crib, and he usually made a drop before he went in. So I figured he would be headed to his car soon. Since I wasn't far from the spot, I figured I would head that way and park behind him. I was a one man army, so I needed to be extra careful. Feeling under the passenger seat in my car, I had to make sure both my guns were still there. After I made sure I was set, I peeled off.

Ten minutes went by, and I was pulling up behind Quan's car. Just like I knew, he was still there. I turned my lights out in my car and slid down in my seat so that no one would see me. Just like clockwork, Quan's stupid ass was walking out of the house with the duffle bag in his hand, with no care in the world. Samaad and I used to always tell him he should wait to leave with everybody else so that he wouldn't be out here alone. This nigga never listens, though.

I hurried and hopped out the car before he saw me, and I closed my car door softly so he wouldn't hear anything. I kneeled down in the back of his car so when he went to open the back door I would be behind him with my gun pointed at the back of his head. When he made it to the car I moved as planned; making sure to stay behind so he couldn't see my face. I also disguised my voice to the best of my ability, so he wouldn't know who I was.

"If you move wrong or make any type of noise, I'll blow your fucking head off. Give me the money and you'll live."

"Come on my nigga, this ain't what you want. Do you know who's money you fucking with?"

"Man, just give me the money. Obviously, I don't give a fuck who the money belongs to. Once I take it, the shit will be mine. You have less than five minutes to give me what I want, or I'm shooting ya ass."

Quan's bitch ass handed me the duffle bag, then I hit that nigga over the head with my gun and he fell to the ground and I took off. Once I got in my car, I sped off so fucking fast. Hopefully, he didn't realize who I was. I was still skeptical about going to my house, so I decided to hit a hotel for a little bit. What the hell, I had money now.

TAJI

Life has been going well for me, and to be honest, I didn't wanna go back to Jersey. Tyreem done bought me a studio and I was more than happy. I was so ready to get this music business on and popping. He and Brodie had a friend that was in the business and he was gone help me get started. It's been a week since Monae had been home and I knew she was going crazy because she couldn't get in touch with me. I changed my number as soon as I dropped her ass off at the airport a week ago. I wasn't fooling with her crazy ass. She even went as far as going to my crib and talking to my dad. He called me checking on me to see when I was coming back. I didn't tell him what my decision was yet. I wanted to get the business on and popping first to show him I can handle my own. My phone started ringing, taking me out of my thoughts. I looked at the screen and saw it was Deja.

"What's good, baby girl, what you up to?"

"Nothing at the moment. Just came from working in the cafeteria, and tomorrow I'm going to register online for my classes."

"That's what's up, Ma. I'm so glad to hear that."

Deja had been having it bad this past couple of days. Bailey said at the beginning she was doing fine, then all of a sudden, she went into a depressed state, so I was trying to keep in touch with her. Making sure she's doing things that she likes to do to keep her mind right.

"Thank you so much, Taji. If it wasn't for your talks and you pushing me, I wouldn't know what to do."

"No thanks needed, Deja. I told you I'd do anything to help."

"I went outside to sit on the bench out front today."

"That's great, Ma."

Deja had been scared to go outside. Ky, Bailey, and Rayne had been trying to get her just to sit out front. She wouldn't, though. All she would say is, 'what if he finds me'. I was so pissed this nigga had her scared like this. Reem and Bailey want me to leave his ass alone, but I couldn't. Every time I looked at her, even though her face was starting to clear up, I got angry all over again.

"Taji, are you ok?" Deja asked.

"Yes, I'm good. Just got caught up in my thoughts, but I'm glad you got some fresh air today. You're starting to make progress, baby."

"After I met with the therapist, I think that helped me a lot."

"That's good, and how's the book coming along?"

"I haven't even really started it yet. Still trynna figure out if I really wanna do it."

"Why are you having doubts about doing it?"

"I don't know, I guess I just don't feel like sharing what I went through with the world yet."

"Which is understandable, just push it to the side until you're ready. Where's Rayne and Eva, your room sound quiet?"

"They at the playroom. Rayne said she was going to go tire Eva out so she can go to bed early tonight."

"Y'all better let my little lady stay up as long as she wants."

Eva was such a cutie. Every time Deja and I would be on FaceTime, she would want to talk to me too.

"Her spoiled little butt needs to be in bed at a decent hour, and not trying to hang with grown folks."

"Little kids are supposed to be spoiled. Wait until you meet Bailey's twins. Man, Reem got them spoiled as hell. They only three and they have everything."

"I know, Ky talks about them all the time. What are you doing in the house so early? Why you never go outside. You're a handsome young guy, and you never talk about having a girlfriend. What's that all about?"

"I'm waiting on a certain special lady, and I don't care how long it takes. I'll be here when she gets ready."

I know Deja know's I'm talking about her, but she always changes the subject. I'm so serious about waiting until she's ready. I know right now is not a good time for her, and that's why I would rather us be friends first.

"Are you gonna be able to come visit me tomorrow, or you have a lot to do like today?"

"Nah, I'm free. Even if I weren't, I'd always make time for you, baby girl."

"OK, so that means I'll see you tomorrow for lunch?"

"Yes, you'll see me tomorrow for lunch. Now get some rest Ma, and I'll talk to you tomorrow, and if you can't sleep, you can call me no matter what time it is."

"Alright and thanks again, Taji."

After we disconnected our call, I continued to lay in the bed in deep thought. Wondering if Deja will be ok after all the pain that she has endured. I know Bailey and Ky are living proof that life gets better, but what if Deja is not as strong as they are. Every time I try to fall back, I just can't do it. You would think I'd known this girl for many years the way I'm feeling her.

"Yo little cuz, what's good?" Reem asked while walking in my room.

"Nothing much, just hung up with Deja. Where are the twins and B at?"

"They over Bro crib with Ky discussing wedding plans. So, Bro on his way over here we about go in the man cave. Have a couple of drinks and buss it up. Samaad about to come through, too.You coming down?"

"Yeah I guess, I ain't doing shit else."

"Are you good? You sound like you're down about something."

"Not really, just thinking about what Deja just asked me. She asked me why I don't have a girl, I'm young and handsome, and I told her because I'm waiting until that special lady is ready. I know she knows I'm talking about her, but she always changes the conversation."

"She's right, you are young, cuz, so have fun. You can't put ya life on hold. Granted I know you want her and I can tell she likes you as well, but she's damaged and it might take her some time. You know I know from experience; I waited for Bailey and it took years. I tried other relationships. They just didn't work for me because she had my heart. So, what I did do, I had friends that I fucked from time to time, and I made sure I let them know what it was from the rip. Not saying you have to do what I did, but you can try to live a little. If it's meant to be, then it will. Trust me, look at me and B now."

I knew Reem was getting sick of having this conversation with me because hell, I was sick of talking about it. I guess the saying the heart wants what the heart wants is a true statement.

SAMAAD

"Man, what the fuck you mean you were robbed? Did you hit Bro or Reem up?"

"Nah man, I hit you first. I didn't wanna bother them, and Reem told us to call you when we need more product. So, I figured I could call you for this."

"No, my nigga, when it comes to that man's cash, you should have called him. Whoever did this must have had it out for you. I say that because why wouldn't they rob the whole trap. They met you at your car like they know your routine. Do you have an idea who this might be?"

"Nah man, I didn't see shit."

"Well, let's go. I'm headed over Reem's crib anyway."

"Nigga, did you let him know you were bringing me? I don't want no problems."

"My dude, you already got problems."

All I could do was shake my head at this stupid motherfucker. We've told Quan time and time again not to walk to his fucking car alone and he stays doing the same bullshit. We headed to my car and we both hopped in. I had already sent Reem a text letting him know what the situation was, and that I was bringing Quan to the crib. As soon as I was about to pull off, my phone started to ring. When I looked down at the number, I saw it was Tee calling.

"What's good, baby girl?"

"Are you coming to stay with me tonight?"

"Yeah. I'll be over in a couple of hours. I'm about to go fuck with Taji in them for a little bit. You gone wait up for me?"

"Probably, but you know where the spare key is if I fall asleep."

"Alright. I'll see you later, baby."

"Ok, and Maady, please be safe out there."

Hearing her say that did something to me. All the chicks I ever dealt with and no one ever told me that before. After I disconnected the call, I peeled off and headed to Reem's crib. After speeding down the highway, driving like a crazy person, I was now pulling up to Reem's house twenty minutes later. Once I parked the car, I sent him a text letting him know me and Quan were out front. As soon as we made it up the steps, Taj was opening up the door.

"Damn nigga, who lumped you the fuck up?" Taj asked while laughing.

"Man, mind ya business, yo."

"Nigga, you better watch ya fucking mouth while talking to me. As a matter of fact, stay ya punk ass the fuck outside until I say you can come in. I'm sick of y'all niggas around here thinking I got bitch in my blood. I got Price in my blood and y'all about to know real soon that we don't fucking play," Taj barked. I looked at Quan's ass and he stayed right on the step like he was told.

"Yo Samaad, can you let Reem know I'm out here?" Quan said right before Taji slammed the door in his face. When we made it in the house and down to the man cave, Bro and Reem were drinking and laughing.

"Hey Samaad, what's good my boy?" Reem said while dapping me up.

"Nothing much, just chilling."

"Where Quan's bitch ass at?"

"Taji punked him and made him sit outside on the step until he's ready to let him in."

Reem and Bro both burst out laughing.

"What he do cuz, to piss you off?"

"I'm sick of these niggas down here talking to me like I got bitch in me. Imma bout to show them I ain't the one. When I start just shooting people just for the hell of it, then they gone think I'm crazy as fuck."

"His bitch ass could stay out there until Samaad ready to go. Maybe why he out there, he can figure out who got my money."

"What money?" Taji asked.

"Quan called me right before I was on my way over here and told me he had a problem. So, I went to the trap to see what was going on and that's when he told me he got robbed. I'm confused why whoever it was didn't rob the whole trap. Instead, they met this nigga at his car and took the duffle bag he had to make the end of the night drop. This shit sounds like they just wanted him, and then they didn't shoot him. I feel like this was done by someone that knew him," I explained. Reem and Bro both were sitting quietly listening to what I was saying.

"Yeah, that shit does sound kind of crazy to me," Reem said.

"You want me to go beat his ass, and see what he knows?" Taji asked.

"Nah, I'll talk to him in a little bit. Right now, let's talk."

"Alright, what's up?"

"I called all y'all here today to let y'all know I want all of you in my wedding." I was shocked. I'd never been asked to be in anyone's wedding, and I was honored.

"You know I'm down, and thanks for asking me."

"I wouldn't have it any other way, Samaad. We like family, my nigga."

After taking a couple of shots and bussing it up with the fellas, it was time for me to head to Tee's house. My ass almost forgot about Quan's ass, but Reem said he had him.

TYREEM

I was pissed off about my money, but I was glad they only targeted him and they didn't rob the whole trap. After making Quan sit outside for hours, I finally went outside to talk with him. Now, I wasn't gone harm him in any way. He was gone owe me whatever amount of money was missing.

"So Quan, tell me what happened, my nigga?"

"I was walking to my car and somebody came up behind me and put a gun to me. Telling me to give him the money."

"His voice didn't sound familiar to you?"

"Nah, not really."

"Well, this is what's gone happen. You will try to get me my money back in a week. If that doesn't work, you will be working your ass off with no pay until all that was lost is returned. You got that?"

Quan looked at me in disbelief, but I didn't give a fuck. He was gone get my money to me one way or another.

"Yeah, man I got you. Are you gone give me ride back to the city?"

"Nope, call an Uber or a cab. My girl on her way home and Imma be here when she gets back."

"Come on Reem, I don't have any money."

"Well, who's fault is that? Shit, I'm down some money too, thanks to you. Now get off my property and figure it out."

I didn't give a damn how he was gone get to where he needed to go and that wasn't my problem. All I know is, he better get going before I beat my money out of his stupid ass. After I said what I said and walked up my steps, I turned to look, making sure his ass started moving. When I made it back in the house, Taji and Bro were still kicking it.

"Where Quan at?" Bro asked.

"I told that nigga to call Uber or a cab. He told me he ain't got no money and I told that nigga get off my property." Taj and Bro both burst out laughing.

"Damn, I thought Taj was bad making that nigga sit outside on the step. Y'all two are hell."

"Man, fuck that nigga. He better find out who the fuck got my damn money, or he gone be working that shit off."

"Hey, what y'all doing down here?" Bailey asked.

"Hey beautiful, I was waiting for you to come home. Where're my boys at?"

"They staying the night at Bro house. Ky didn't want me to take them."

I walked over to her, pulled her in for a hug, and palmed her ass.

"Oh really, Ky must have known I was drinking tonight and I didn't want no interruptions."

"Stop Reem, what ya nasty ass did, you forget we are not alone."

"Fuck them, they in my crib. If they don't like it they can leave."

"You ain't said nuttin but a word, my nigga. I'm out," Bro said, getting up from the couch.

"Yeah, I'm going to bed. I'll check you out tomorrow, cuz," Taji said. Once they both left out, I locked the door to my man cave, and pulled Bailey over to the bar.

"Come on baby, have a couple of shots with ya man."

I poured her a double shot and then myself. We sat, talked, and drank for a little while, before I bent her sexy ass over the back of the couch and fucked the shit out of her. When we both got to drinking, we always ended our night fucking like porn stars.

BAILEY

One Month Later

The center had been hectic lately, and we'd been swamped with work. I hadn't even been able to plan my wedding like Reem wanted me to do. Ky and I had discharges and admissions like crazy. It was like when one person left, another came. We enjoyed every bit of it, but we were considering hiring more people so her and I could be home a little more. There was a knock at my office door taking me out of my thoughts.

"Come in," I yelled.

"Hey Bailey, how are you? Have you heard from Rayne yet?" Deja asked.

"No baby, not yet. Ky said she was gone call her mother today to see if she's heard anything from her."

Rayne had been gone for three days. She said she was going to the store and never came back. We had been noticing funny activity with her for the past couple of weeks. These women are grown, and they can come and go as they please. We just ask them not to bring the drama near here. So, if they are gone to meet their abuser, we ask them to go far away from here.

"I'm so mad at her Bailey, and I hope she didn't go back to him."

"Deja, Rayne is a grown ass woman and she might not have been ready to leave Terrell. We can give y'all all the advice in the world, but it's up to y'all what y'all chose to do with it. We take y'all in, but we can't make y'all stay."

"I know. I just hope her and Eva are ok."

"Hey y'all, what's up?" Ky asked while walking in the office.

"Hey mama, how are you?"

"I'm good tired, but good."

"Hello Ky, have you contacted Rayne's mama yet?"

"No, but I can call right now while we all are in here."

Ky pulled her phone out and dialed the number. Deja and I just sat and listened until she hung the phone up.

"Her mom said she hadn't seen her in a couple of days, and somebody needs to come get Eva," Ky said as soon as she disconnected her call.

"OH MY GOD! Something happened to her." Deja jumped up and ran over to me crying.

"Don't cry baby, we don't know what happened yet. Let me call the hospitals, and see if they have her," I assured Deja while rubbing her back.

I knew something wasn't right because Rayne would never leave Eva. Either something bad had happened to her or Terrell was holding her prisoner. Usually we didn't get deeply involved in stuff like this, but we got attached to Deja and Rayne in such little time.

"I'm gone go and pick Eva up and she'll stay with Bro and me until we find Rayne. Bailey, call the police and tell them that she's been missing for over forty-eight hours. Also let them know her history with Terrell, so that way if they don't answer the door when they get to the house, they can enter. Don't you worry Deja, we are going to find out what happened." After I calmed Deja down, she left out and went to her room.

"Do you think she'll be ok?"

"Yeah, she'll be fine. I just think she grew to love Rayne in this little bit of time. I hope to God everything is ok with her."

"Me too, but this shit doesn't feel right, Ky. She would never leave Eva with her mom for more than a couple of hours."

"I know, but we gotta think positive and pray about it. Go ahead and call the police station, and when you're finished, take a ride with me to go get Eva."

I did as I was told and called the police station and told them everything they needed to know. I even told them that she was just in the hospital almost two months ago for Terrell beating her. By the time I was done with the call, they had assured me that they would be right on it. They also made me aware that if she was at the house alive and well, it wouldn't be anything they can do. Rayne would have to do a restraining order, and that's something that she and Deja wouldn't do when they first came here.

"Ok, that's done. Detective Lee took my number and yours. He said he would get back to us as soon as he hears anything. He also said to give him a call if we hear anything first."

"Alright, come on let's go."

Ky and I hopped in my car. We plugged the address into the GPS and headed to get Eva. Twenty minutes passed by and we were pulling up to a nice townhouse. I parked the car and we both jumped out. Ky walked up on the step and knocked on the door while I stood behind her. This evil ass lady came to the door with a cigarette in her hand, looking like she had been drinking. Now if drinking is ya thing, that's fine, but you shouldn't do it when you have a small child in your presence.

"Hello, How can I help you?"

"Hello, I just talked to you like about forty-five minutes ago. I'm Ky from the center."

"Oh yeah, I remember. Exactly what kind of center is that you girls work at."

"A center to help young ladies like Rayne better themselves."

We didn't get all into details about the center because we didn't know much about her mother. Most young ladies talk about their mothers with pride when they are good mothers. Rayne only told us the basics, which led us to believe they weren't close at all.

"Well, I hope it does her some good. I worked my ass off to get her through school and her ass dropped out. I don't want shit to do with her, always running behind that damn boy. You see how her unfit ass is, just left her daughter here."

"Ma'am, did Rayne ever explain to you why she didn't finish school?"

"Nope, and I didn't care to hear what her sorry ass excuse was."

I didn't know about Ky but I was sick of sitting here talking to this old drunk. Meeting her explained why Rayne kept a lot of shit from her. Hell, she might be the reason she was so fast to move out with Terrell.

"Alright, well I'm here to get Eva. Can I ask you a question?"

"Come on young lady, hurry it up. I'm missing my show."

"How come you didn't report Rayne missing when she didn't come to pick Eva up. Isn't that kind of unusual."

"Look lady, it's none of your business why I do what I do. Let me go get the baby bag so you can get off my damn step."

Ky held her arms out to Eva and she went right to her. She looked nice and clean, but she didn't seem like the little happy baby we're used to.Maybe she was missing Rayne. Once the old hag came back to the door, I snatched the bag out of her hand and we left off her step. Tonight, I was gone pray that we found Rayne safe. I wouldn't want Eva to grow up without her mother.

DEJA

Not knowing where Rayne was had me in my feelings. Nothing felt good about any of this. I told her not to go, but she wouldn't listen to me, and there was no one to tell. Bailey and Ky weren't our mothers and we weren't locked up. We can come and go as we please, we just had to be in at a certain time. That night Rayne missed curfew, I had a feeling she wasn't coming back. When Eva started asking for Terrell, Rayne felt bad for keeping her away from her daddy. So, she set up a date for them to meet up to see Eva. Then she started sneaking out after curfew. I knew he was gone reel her back in. The knock on my door brought me out of my thoughts. I jumped up off the bed and answered the door.

"Hey Ma, what's up?" Taji said while pulling me in for a hug. Taji and I had been kicking it since I'd been here and he's been every bit of amazing to me. He likes me a whole lot and I can tell, but I ain't ready for nothing serious. He knows that and he said he's going to wait for me to be ready.

"Hello Taji, what brings you here?"

"I'm about to sing a couple of songs in the auditorium, and this all-girl group I'm thinking about managing is gone sing a couple of songs as well. Remember the amateur night starts tonight."

"Oh. Damn, I did forget. This shit with Rayne is getting to me, so I haven't really been in the loop."

"What's up with her, have they talk to her?"

"No, and her mom had Eva for two days. Ky and Bailey just went to get her because her mom didn't want to keep the baby."

"Wow, that's wild as hell. How you not want your granddaughter?"

"Right, this shit is crazy and I hope she's ok."

"She'll be fine baby. Come on, come watch the show with me. You need to get out of this room." Taji was right I needed to get my mind off of things and music would work.

"Ok, let me run to the bathroom real quick."

I went to the bathroom, fixed my hair, threw some lipgloss on, and headed out the door with Taji following behind me. Once we made it to the show, the girls were already on stage singing and dancing. Taji stood behind me and pulled me in. My back was now resting on his chest. It felt so good being in his arms, not to mention he smelled so damn good.

"They sound good, don't they?" Taji asked.

"Yes, they sound real dope. Where did you find them?"

"I had auditions at the studio last week, and they were one of the acts that I was interested in."

"Oh ok, you doing big things, Mr. Price."

"I'm trying, baby girl. You know music is my life, so I'm gone try my best to live my dream. You ready to live it with me?"

"As soon as I get my mind right, I'll be ready."

"Cool and I'll be right here waiting for you," Taji said while kissing the back of my neck.

After the girls were done there second song, they called Taji to the stage. I clapped and screamed like I was his biggest fan. He started singing *Ask Of You* by Raphael Saadiq. I knew he only sang this song because it had my name in it. I swear Taji was something else and his voice was amazing. I swayed my hips from side to side, enjoying the music.

I'll be right there on time, it's your place or mine just show me the place

I really love you, I really love you I love you Deja I love you Deja

Once he said the chorus part with my name in it, I was all smiles. I swear this man was doing everything in his power to get me to want him, and he was winning. I was just scared shitless and worried about it being too soon to be in any type of relationship. Then that's when thoughts would come to mind. Am I done with Jace? I mean, I think I'm done with him. But am I strong enough to keep it moving if I was to run into him? See, there was plenty of shit I needed to figure out before I moved on in life. Taji was a great man. I'm just damaged and before I mess his life up, I would rather just be alone. Then I looked at Bailey and Ky's relationship and I wanted to be with a man that loved me wholeheartedly just like theirs did. I figure I would talk to the both of them and ask their advice on this. After Taji got done singing, he made his way back over to me.

"What you know about that song?"

"Shit, I was about to ask you the same thing," I said and we both laughed.

"What you wanna do now?" Taji asked me.

"Can we walk around the little park out front."

"Sure, anything you wanna do, mama."

Taji grabbed my hand and we headed out the back door. Our conversations and walks in the parks are everything, and to be honest with y'all, most of my days I look forward to seeing Taji. He just makes sure I'm on the right path. I swear I met a new family when I met him, Bailey, Reem, Ky, and Brodie.

KYLAYDA

When I found out that Eva was with her Grandmom my heart broke instantly. I knew this wasn't going to be a good outcome. Talking to Rayne and getting to know her, we knew she would not have left Eva. I looked in the backseat and Eva was knocked out sleeping. I didn't even bother to call Brodie to let him know what was going on, I knew he wouldn't turn Eva away.

My name is Kylayda Monroe, formerly known as Kylayda Sanchez-Brooks, and I was born and raised in Atlanta Georgia. My daddy raised me alone because my no-good ass mama walked out on us. I was now twenty-nine years old and married to the man of my dreams, Brodie Monroe. Pulling into our driveway, I noticed his car wasn't there yet. I hurried and locked the car up, and grabbed Eva with all the bags I got out of the car. I didn't know how long she was gone be with us, but I made sure she had everything she needed. I was struggling to get the front door open when Brodie pulled up.

"Baby, what are you doing and what's all that stuff?" he asked walking up behind me. He didn't notice I had a sleeping Eva in my arms until he made it all the way up the steps.

"Why you didn't call me and tell me you were bringing Eva home?

I would have met you here so I can help you. Why she got all this shit like she moving in?"

"Can we get in the house first, Brodie? Then we can talk about it."

Brodie opened the door, then grabbed all the bags, and followed me into the house.

"Where do you want all this stuff at?"

"You can bring it up to the twins' rooms. Imma lay her in their room, and grab the monitor."

"Are you sure she gone be ok in there alone. She not used to us, Ky."

"Alright, well she can lay on our couch that's in our room."

"Ok, well when you are done lying her down, meet me downstairs so we can talk."

I took Eva in our room, took her clothes off and put a little night-gown on her, then laid her down. Once I made sure she was safe I met my husband downstairs.

"So, what's going, baby? I can see the sadness in your eyes."

"Rayne is missing, and it's not looking good."

"What happen, and why you say it doesn't look good."

"She's been gone from the center for like a week, but she left Eva with her mom two days ago. I know she would not have left her with that lady for more than a couple of hours. The bitch even said she didn't want her, so she wishes someone would come pick her up. How could she be so cruel like that? Eva is such a beautiful baby. Then I asked her did she report her daughter missing and she said no, what for."

"Wow, that bitch needs her ass kicked. Well lil mama is cool with staying here as long as you want her to. Now come over here and show your man some love." I walked over to Bro and he pulled me into his arms. "You always let this job stress you out. Just relax, and everything will work out. As far as Rayne, I hope she is ok."

"Thank you baby for always being here for me. I've been going through shit since we first started out, and you've been by my side for it all. I'm so proud to be your wife," I cooed while pulling Brodie in for a kiss. Bro and I had been together for well over five years now, and we had been through some shit. Not the usual relationship shit, just him dealing with a broken woman like me. It ain't been easy. But the love he has for me, he stuck it out and now here I am, Mrs. Kylayda Monroe.

"Mmmmm, girl don't be kissing me like that. We got company tonight," Brodie chuckled.

"So, because we got company I can't get none?"

"Nope, come on and let's go to bed."

"Let's take a shower together first, then we can go to bed."

"You think your hot ass so slick. You know it's on when we get in this shower," Brodie laughed and grabbed my hand and led the way.

Once we made it to the bathroom, I stripped out of my clothes then helped my husband out of his. I then turned the water on and ran it to the temperature we liked. Once we were satisfied, we both jumped in.

"Do you think you can handle him?" Brodie asked while looking down at his hard dick.

I ran my hands down his chest and eased them down to his dick. I slowly began stroking my best friend just the way he liked, right before I dropped to my knees and took him all the way in my mouth.

"Mmm Hmm, do you like that baby. Am I sucking it right?"

"Ahh....fuck. Yes Ky, just like that baby," Brodie yelled out.

I knew he was coming close to his climax, but I wasn't ready for him to cum just yet. I got up, grabbed his face, pulled it to mine, and kissed him passionately. Brodie lifted me up and I wrapped my legs around his waist and started griding on his dick. Light moans escaped my mouth as I enjoyed the sensation of his dick rubbing against my clit.

"Brodie baby, please put it in," I cried as I craved for him to enter me.

He smirked and slowly pushed into me. Once he was in all the way, he leaned me against the shower wall and gave me nice, long, deep strokes. I had to hold my screams in because I didn't want to wake Eva. My husband gave me the business, as usual. I knew after this I was gone be out for the night. We explored each other until the water turned cold.

JACE

It's been a whole damn month and I still hadn't seen my girl. Yeah, a nigga was going the fuck crazy. Sitting in this hotel room still wondering where the fuck she disappeared to, I found myself drinking and snorting coke trying to get over her. The shit was getting out of hand. The money I took from Quan that night would have lasted me a long time if I didn't pick up two habits.

"You good, baby?" This chick Lola that I met at the bar last night asked.

"Yeah I'm cool, Ma."

"Are you sure? If not, I can make you feel better," she said while she straddled me.

"I'm sure, Ma. I just got some shit on my mind, that's all."

"What's on ya mind? Maybe I can help you out?"

"Money, I need to make some moves to get some cash."

"Jace, if I ask you something, will you keep it real with me?"

"Depends on what you wanna know."

"Well, damn, I guess I can't get mad at you are being honest," Lola chuckled.

"What you wanna know, Ma?" I asked while playing with her pretty, long hair.

"I can tell you're a street nigga, so what's up with you. Why are you staying in a hotel? Are you hiding from someone, and why are you low on funds?"

"Nah, I actually just lost someone that's dear to me almost two months ago. So, I don't wanna be in the house right now, that's all. The shit has actually been having me in a fucked up mind space, which causes me to miss out on the money." Not telling her everything and not wanting to talk about this anymore I pulled her in for a kiss. She pulled away and smiled at me.

"Don't be trying to kiss me to shut me up. I wasn't done talking." I grabbed her hand and put it on my dick.

"You feel him, he ain't trynna talk right now."

"Mmmmmm, I thought he didn't want me to take care of him."

"I guess he changed his mind. Come and show him some love."

Lola was already ass naked, so she lifted up and slid down on my mans nice and slow the way I liked. Watching her titties bounce while she rode my dick had me so fucking turned on. Lola was so fucking beautiful with A1 pussy. What rubbed me the wrong way about her was meeting her in the bar. That shit made me wonder was this some shit she did all the time. Even though she claimed she didn't and I was her first one night stand, these hoes don't be loyal so I didn't know what to think. Lola was starting to speeding up the pace and I felt her pussy muscles contracting on my dick. I knew she was about to bust, and so was I.

"You ready to cum on this dick, Ma?" She didn't need to answer me because the way her eyes were rolling in the back of her head, I knew what it was.

"Mmm, hmm, keep moving just like that."

"I'm about to cum Jace, I'm about to cum."

"I'm about to cum, too. Where you want this nut at?"

"I'm about to taste it," Lola's nasty ass said. She jumped off my dick after she busted her nut, then took me into her mouth and finished me off.

"Ahhhhh, fuck!" I yelled while shooting my seeds down her throat.

Lola looked up at me smiling. I swear she was beautiful, but she wasn't Deja. She was keeping my mind off Deja, but I still missed her so fucking much. Yeah, maybe I shouldn't have been hitting on her, but hell, maybe she should have fucking listened. Lola eased her way back on top of me.

"So, what's on your agenda today?"

"I'm trynna make some money moves today. I need to get back on my shit. What about you? What you gone be up to?"

"Nothing I'm free all day today, so I'm probably just gone chill at home. You're welcome to come over if you're free after you handle your business. I can cook you dinner if you would like."

"Yeah that's cool Ma, I might be a little late, but I'll be there."

After we talked a little more, we got up and showered, then left out of the room.

* * *

The drugs and drinking brought me off my game big time. I even stopped following Tee's hoe ass around to see if she knew where Deja was. I know what y'all wondering, how the hell this nigga just get up today with Deja on his mind. To be honest with y'all, some days I'm cool but others, I am so pissed off she just left me. Does she understand how much she hurt me? I think that's the main thing that hurt me the worst is that she didn't even care how I felt when she left. My whole life is so fucked up right now. A nigga drinking and sniffing coke like it's cool, and not to mention I'm broke as shit. I was hungry as shit, so I decided to stop at Popeye's to get some chicken. I parked my car, then jumped out; when I walked in, I saw Quan chilling all by himself. So, I walked over to say what's up.

"Yo my nigga, what's good with you?" I said while dapping him up.

"Hey J, I ain't seen you around in a minute. What you been up to?"

"Nothing, trynna make moves. Hold up, let me get my food, then I'll come kick it with you."

I walked over ordered me a three-piece, red beans and rice, and sweet tea. Once I had my food, I grabbed some napkins then walked over to where Quan was.

"So, man what's been good with you?"

"Nothing at all, just trynna maintain, and figure out some money moves. How are you doing out in these streets? You still deal with Reem and Bro?"

"Yeah, man but I fucked around and got robbed a while ago, and that nigga got me working my ass off without being paid. I'm about sick of those niggas, though, and his little cousin, I wanna body his corny ass."

Well I knew for sure they didn't suspect me of robbing him, which was a good thing. Then an idea popped in my head, I figured maybe he could help me make some money moves since he was low on cash himself.

"Well, you already know I didn't like that nigga from the rip. Y'all always wanted to know why I didn't. He just rubbed me the wrong way, his vibe was off to me."

"It seems like every time I see that nigga, we get into it on some bullshit."

"Fuck that soft ass nigga. But check this, I'm trynna make some money moves and you sound like you need to do the same." Quan looked at me like he was ready for me to start talking.

"So, what's the plan?"

"Not sure yet, but soon as I figure some shit out we can make it happen."

"Alright, well you got my number, right?"

"Yeah, I got it."

"Ok, true, well let me get out of here and make sure you hit me up. I'm serious Jace, I need a come up for real."

"I got you. Don't even worry about that."

Quan and I dapped each other up and he headed out of the door. Twenty minutes later, I finished my food, then headed out of the door.

DEJA

Last night, I enjoyed spending time with Taji, but when he left, I was all alone. Being all alone made me realize how much I missed my mother, and today was gone be the day I went to visit her. I wanted to tell her everything that went down between Jace and me, but I knew I couldn't do it alone. So I figured I would call Tiombe. I pulled my phone out and dialed her number, and she picked up on the first ring.

"Hey mama, what you doing?" I asked.

"Nothing just lying here. What's wrong?"

"I wanna go see my mom today and wanted to know can you come with me?"

"Now you know you didn't even have to ask. What time you wanna go?"

"I just got up and about to head to the shower now. So, maybe in an hour or two."

"Ok that's cool, see you in a little bit."

After I hung up, I got out of the bed and headed to my closet to find something to wear. I had plenty of clothes thanks to Ky, Tiombe, and Taji. See when I left Jace, I left everything behind. I had to get all new things. It was a good thing I still had the key. So, one day Taji and Samaad went there and got my purse which had all my important shit inside. I even had them get my little bag I had hiding underneath the floor in the closet. I had money in there saved for a rainy day.

Yeah, I had plans on getting out of that fucked up relationship. I just didn't know when, and how; after what I endured, my mind was now made up that I would never go back to him. Do I think about him? Yes, I do, shit he was all the fuck I knew. It's going to take me a little bit longer to get him fully out of my mind, but I am sure I'm done with all of that. Deciding on a pair of blue jeans, and a burnt orange crop sweater, I laid it out on the bed, then walked into the bathroom and turned the shower on to the temperature I like.

I hopped in, letting the water run down my body for a little while. I lathered my rag with my Dove body wash. After washing and rinsing my body a couple of times, I felt refreshed. I shut the water off, then grabbed my towel, dried off, and wrapped it around my waist. Once I made it back to my room, I put my Bluetooth speaker on, then started my playlist. Music has gotten me through a whole lot of rough days and nights. I even named my playlist 'The Story of My Life'. I walked over to the dresser to grab my lotion to moisturize my skin. *You Ain't Shit by Sonta* blared through the speakers. I sang while I was getting myself together.

I used to wanna be your everything, but now I don't wanna be nothing

Cuz you ain't shit, boy you ain't shit, and leaving you alone I dodged a bullet

Cuz you ain't shit boy you ain't shit, and ima need you to keep your distance

Not seeing any bruises on my body made me feel so good. A smile crept up on my face knowing that I was in a better place in life. I knew I wasn't exactly where I needed to be, but I was in a better space. The first step was getting out, and that's what I did. The hard part will be staying away, and as of now, I'm doing good. Only because I've been keeping myself inside. It's time for me to go out and find a job and maybe go to school. Staying in here hiding out from the real world because I didn't wanna run into Jace was getting old.

Yeah, when I run into him Imma be shook, but I believe that'll be the only way I know I'm done with him. The music stopped, which means Tiombe was calling me. I jumped up off the bed and grabbed my phone. Tee had left a text message letting me know she was on her way. I laid the phone back down and hurried to get myself dressed. Once I was completely dressed, I looked myself over in the mirror, and noticed I'd picked up a little weight. Another smile crept up on my face; and I guess y'all can say I was feeling myself. I slid my feet into a pair of black nine west booties and sprayed some Paris Hilton perfume on. Then I fluffed out my naturally curly hair a little with my fingers, before I headed out front to wait for Tiombe. Before I made it to the door, I stopped by Bailey and Ky's office to let them know I was stepping out for a minute. The door was already open, so I peeked my head in.

"Good morning, y'all!" I said in excitement.

"Hey beautiful, you look cute," Ky said.

"I'm going to go see my mom. I wanted to let y'all know before I headed out."

"You need us to tag along?" Bailey asked.

"Nah, I'm good, Tiombe is on her way."

"Alright be safe, and tell Tee we said hello," Ky said. I told them ok then headed out the door. As soon as I got out front, Tee was already pulling up.

"Hey chicka!" I said while leaning over to kiss her cheek.

"Hey mama, you look so pretty today."

"Thanks, and so do you. Glowing and what not, let me find out."

"Find out what bish, don't start that pregnant shit." I've been picking with Tee and Maady lately, telling them they gone have a baby soon.

"So, what's been going on, BFF?"

"Nothing much, school and Maady."

"Y'all getting close as hell lately. Have y'all made it official yet?"

"Yeah, we talked about it last night. I'm really feeling him Deja, and he makes me better. I don't even be wanting to hang out in the streets no more."

"Ayyyyye, sounds like my bro put it on you," I said while laughing.

"Shut up crazy. So, you ready to tell your mom about Jace?"

"To be honest Tee, yes I'm ready. I'm finally at a point in my life where I wanna move on. I can't stay stuck in my past, but you really know what I want?"

"What do you really want?"

"I wanna see him. I feel like that's the only way I'll know that I'm over him."

"I don't think that's a good idea, boo."

"I'm not going to go looking for him, Tee. I know eventually, I'll run into him soon. See, the only reason I haven't run into him yet because I had shut down and refused to go outside. We in the same city, it's bound to happen soon."

"Well, I hope when it happens you're not alone."

We were so into our conversation I didn't even realize we were pulling up in front of my mom's house. Tiombe parked the car and we both got out. I was kind of hesitant, but I was here already, so I needed to get it done and over with. Once we made it on the porch, I knocked on the door a couple of times. The door opened and my mother was standing there looking at me like she was shocked. She grabbed me and pulled me in for a hug.

"Baby, where have you been? The only thing that kept me from filing a missing person report was Tee telling me you were ok." Yeah I had Tee keep in touch with my mom so she wouldn't report me as missing.

"I'm sorry mama, I had a lot going on in my life."

"It's ok, you here now. Come on in and talk to me." My mama was so calm, but I knew she was about to do a whole 360 when I told her about her precious Jace.

"Hey auntie!" Tee said.

"Hey baby, your mom just called me a little while ago. She told me about this new boyfriend you got. When you gone bring him to meet me?"

"Real soon, I gotta see when he's free," Tee assured her. We all made in the house and sat in the living room. It was an awkward silence until Tee said something.

So, auntie what you been up to?"

"Nothing much, working, sleeping, and worried about my baby."

"Well mama, I've been away for a month and a week. Trying to get my life back in order, and to get away from Jace." She looked at me kind of confused, which caused me to hesitate. But Tiombe gave me a head nod, telling me to continue with my story.

"What you mean staying away from Jace?"

"Mama, Jace has been abusing me." As soon as those words left my mouth, the tears started to roll down my face.

"Oh my God! Baby, why didn't you tell me? I'm so sorry I wasn't around to help you."

"I was scared, mama. He had me messed up physically and mentally, but I'm doing a lot better."

"Where is he, Deja? Why isn't he in jail?"

"Mama, I don't know where he is. I haven't seen him since the day he beat me so bad I needed medical attention. That's when Tee's boyfriend and a friend of mine found me and took me the domestic violence center." My mom was crying her eyes out. The reaction I was getting from her was different than I expected.

"I wish you would have come to me. I know I loved him and praised him, but if I had known he was hurting my pride and joy, I would have killed him."

I got up from where I was sitting, walked over to my mom, and fell in her arms. We hugged for what seemed like forever.

"Mama, I've missed you so much, but the girls at the center have treated me so well. They've helped me get back on my feet. I'm not ready to leave there just yet. But when I do, I might need to stay with you for a little while."

"You know your always welcome, baby. You can come now if you want to."

"Not yet mama, I don't think I'm ready for that just yet. Give me a couple of weeks to a month, then maybe."

"Auntie we just now getting her to come outside. She shut the whole world out, but she is getting back slowly but surely," Tiombe said, breaking the silence.

"Listen baby, I don't care how much I liked Jace. A man should never hit a woman. If he loved you, he wouldn't have been hurting you, and when I see his ass, I'm beating him the fuck up."

Tee and I burst out laughing. What my mama said was funny, but I knew she was telling the truth. We continued to talk and laugh for hours. She even made us something to eat. I was so happy to see her and now I was gone make it my business to keep in touch with her more.

KYLAYDA

It's been two days since Bailey and I went to get Eva from her dumb ass grandmom's house. Brodie and I were enjoying Eva's company, but I was still worried about Rayne. The detectives still hadn't got back to me, so at this point, yes I was thinking negative thoughts. My phone started to ring taking me out of my thoughts.

"Hello Lexi's Helping Hands, this is Ky speaking."

"Hello Mrs. Ky, I'm Detective Lee and I'm the one handling Rayne King's case. I'm calling to inform you that her body was found last night inside of a trunk in an empty lot; we also wanted you to know we have Terrell Banks in custody for her murder."

I was lost for words. I knew what the outcome would be, but to actually hear it hurt my heart.

"Ok, Detective Lee, has anyone identified the body?"

"Yes, her mother did. But she said we could do whatever we want with the body, she doesn't have no money to be burying her." I thought to myself, *wow, her mother is a piece of shit.*

"Alright, I will call her mother and talk to her. My husband and I will take care of the arrangements, and thanks so much for contacting me."

As soon as I hung the phone up, I started crying. I couldn't catch my breath. I was hyperventilating and everything. This shit was a hard pill to swallow. He left this baby motherless, and her mom didn't give a damn about burying her.

"Oh my God! Ky, what's wrong?" Bailey asked walking into the office.

"They found her body sis. He brutally beat her, then put her in the trunk of the car and left the car in a vacant lot. Then took his sorry ass home like he didn't do shit. I'm so glad the cops locked his black ass up."

Bailey pulled me in for a hug and we cried like this was our child. I swear this shit gets personal sometimes, but we had to get our shit straight so we could break the news to Deja.

"We have to be strong for Eva and Deja."

"Her Mom told the detectives they could do whatever with her body because she doesn't have no money to bury her. I told the detective that Bro and I would take care of the arrangements, but you best believe I'm giving her sorry ass mom a piece of my mind."

We both sat in silence, trying to get our mind together before we break the news to Deja.

"Alright you ready to go do this?"

"Not really, but we have to. This shit is going to break her heart."

"They were beginning to be just like us. We needed each other the get through our hard times. I know she has Tee, but it ain't nothing like someone who can relate to what you've been through."

"Well, she'll always have us. Come on, let's go."

Bailey and I got up and headed to Deja's room in slow motion. Once we made it to her door, I knocked a couple of times. When she finally opened the door, we could see she had been sleeping.

"Hey Ky and B, what's up?"

"Hey love bug, can we come in and talk to you for a minute?"

"Now you know y'all don't have to ask that question, y'all do own the place." I gave her a weak little smile, then we walked in.

"Deja I just got off the phone with the detective that's handling Rayne's case. They found her dead today, brutally beaten inside of the trunk of a car in a vacant lot."

"NOOOOOOOOOOO!" Deja screamed letting out a gut-wrenching cry. She almost fell to the floor, but I ran over and caught her.

"Calm down baby, before you make yourself sick."

"Why did he do that to her? Why did he hurt her like that?" I sat on her bed holding her and rocking her. Until she broke away from my hold, "I need to go I need to take a walk. I don't wanna be here right now."

"Where you wanna go, Deja? I don't think you should be alone right now."

"I'll be fine, I just need some air."

I really didn't want her to leave here angry like this, but I knew it wasn't any keeping her here. I was just finna call Taji about what's going on and hopefully he can catch up with her.

"Come on Deja, don't leave here like this, baby girl. I'll call Taji to come get you if you want me to," Bailey tried to reason with her.

"I don't care what you two say, I'm leaving for a little while. I need some air," Deja said while throwing a sweat suit and some sneakers on. I could see all in her face that she was fucked up over this.

"Deja, please be safe out there and call us if you need us. Come on Bailey, let's give her some space." Before I left out of the room, I kissed Deja on her cheek and walked out.

"Where do you think she's going, Ky?" Bailey asked while we were headed to our office.

"I have no idea, but call Taj and tell him what's going on, so, he can try and stop her." I went back to my office and took care of some paperwork.

"You should go ahead home with Eva," Bailey said.

"I'm good Imma stay here a little longer so Eva can play with the kids. How are you holding up? I know how close you've gotten to Rayen since she's been here. My feelings are so hurt and how they found her is so fucked up. I want that nigga dead Ky, and you know I don't even talk like that."

"I know baby, you're angry right now. Hell I am too, and if he weren't in police custody, I would say come on let's go get that motherfucker."

I gave Bailey a little smirk. I did need to leave, but I knew I would have been home in my feelings. I was gone stay here and tend to our other clients and make this day productive.

TAJI

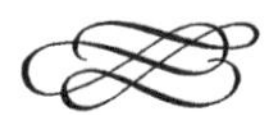

I was in the studio helping my new girl group lay a couple of tracks when Bailey called me and told me what happen to Rayne. I was really fucked up behind hearing that shit, and the first thing that came to mind was how Deja was dealing with it. Bailey told me she said she was leaving the center, she needed to get some air. She didn't have a car and she didn't call me, so I wasn't feeling her walking anywhere. So, I pulled my phone out to call Samaad to make sure he and Tee weren't picking her up. I pulled my phone out, dialed his number, and he picked up on the first ring.

"Yo Samaad, are you and Tee picking Deja up?"

"Nah, why you ask that? Is she good?"

"No, man, Bailey just called me and told me that they found Rayne dead. Now Deja tripping talking about she needs to get out and get some fresh air. You know she doesn't have no car and I ain't feeling her walking around by herself."

Deja hadn't seen Jace yet. She'd been staying in the center unless we get her to come out. Usually she just wanted to stay inside. The closest we got her to go outside was when she's walking around the building. Tee did tell me that she finally went to see her mother, which I thought was great news.

"Well, what you ready to do?"

"I'm about to take a ride to the center hoping I catch her before she leaves."

"Alright cool, do you need me to come?"

"Nah I'm good, if I need you, I'll hit you up."

After I assured Samaad I was good, I grabbed my car keys, told the girls I would be back, then I walked out of the door. Once I made it to my car, I jumped in and peeled off. I was speeding my ass off, breaking every law in Atlanta. I knew I had to hurry up, because if Deja was walking, I was sure to run right into her. In ten minutes, I was pulling up to the center, I shot B a text and she told me that Deja had left already. So, I rode around the center a couple of times and she was nowhere in sight. How the hell did her ass move that damn fast? I pulled my phone out and dialed her number. *Come on baby, please pick up,* was all I kept saying to myself, but she never picked up. I called Tee so she could call Deja's mom to see if she made it over there, but she said she hadn't seen her. Then she made Tee assure her that she would call her the minute we found her. After riding around looking for Deja for another hour, I just gave up, and headed back to my studio, feeling defeated. It took me ten minutes to get back to the studio. When I entered, all the girls were gone, except one. She was singing the prettiest song I've ever heard; I didn't bother her, I just sat and listened until she was finished. Once she was done, I clapped and smiled at her.

"Damn Kaci, that shit was fiyah, Ma."

"You really like it, Taji?"

"Yes, where you get that from?"

"It was a song I wrote a while back after my mama died."

"You should record it solo after you finish the album with the group."

"Oh My God! Taji, thank you so much," she said while she ran into my arms to hug me. Once we separated we looked into each other's eyes. *Man Taj, what the fuck you doing,* I said to myself. Before I could move out of the way, Kaci kissed my lips, and her lips were so soft I couldn't help but to kiss her back.

"Yo cuz, did you hear what happen to Rayne?" Reem asked, busting in the door. Kaci and I jumped and ended our kiss. Reem looked at me with a stupid smirk on his face.

"Hey what's up, cuz. Kaci, I'll see you tomorrow afternoon when you come for studio time."

"Alright Taji and thanks again," Kaci smiled and left out the door.

"Sorry man, I didn't mean to interrupt."

"You good, that shit shouldn't have gone down anyway."

"Yeah I agree, don't mix business with pleasure."

"I know and I don't want nobody but Deja anyway. Speaking of Deja, man I'm so pissed I can't find her ass, and yeah that's fucked up about Rayne. I swear it's so many fuck boys out here beating on women."

"Yeah man, that shit is real crazy. The way he fucking left her in the trunk of the car, he lucky the cops got his bitch ass. Have you tried calling Deja's phone?"

"Yeah man and she keeps sending me straight to voicemail."

"She hurt right now cuz, just give her some space."

"Imma try to, but I'm gone go looking for her ass tomorrow if she doesn't answer me."

"Look at ya ole sucka for love ass."

"I know you ain't talking, nigga."

"Shut ya ass up. But check this, have you called ya pops?"

"Yeah man a couple of days ago, and we got into it. I ain't about to keep arguing about my life, Reem."

"I get it cousin, I really do. But at the end of the day, he still ya pops. Just answer the phone when he hit you again. He called me this morning fussing about you not wanting to talk to him. I explained to him that you are busy in your studio. Then he cursed me out for letting you come down here starting this music shit. I told him how good you are in it, and how proud I am of you. I also told him you got ya hustle from us and he shouldn't knock what you do, as long as you still bringing money in the family."

"I'll hit him up tomorrow, and thanks for talking to him for me, cousin. I really appreciate you for letting me stay with you, helping me get the studio, and helping me get it running."

"No problem, just remember you in charge of all the music for my wedding."

"No doubt, you know I got you. What you ready to get into?"

"I'm about to head home. I just thought I'd come check you out since I was in the area. Baby girl that you was kissing on is bad as hell, but she doesn't look better than Deja," Reem said.

"Nigga, you crazy for that one," I chuckled.

Since the studio was empty and no one had no time booked for today, I was leaving right behind Reem; tonight was gone be long for me, because I already knew if I didn't hear from Deja my ass ain't gone be able to sleep.

BAILEY

Finally home lying in my bed, today has been a rough day for me. Hearing the shit that happened to Rayne had me in my feelings. Some of these stories bring me back to what had happened to me, and I'm always thanking God for letting me live. Yeah, Rayne was wrong for going to see him, but she didn't know he would do that to her. Especially when the kids are involved. I knew back then that Maleek would never hurt the twins, so if he were still around and wanted to see them, I probably would take them. I don't know about going alone, but I would never keep him away from his kids. People judge women that go through domestic violence every day, but you'll never know how deep it is, unless you were a victim.

"Hey baby, what you in here thinking about?" Reem asked walking into our bedroom.

"Thinking about what happened to Rayne."

Reem stripped out of his clothes, climbed into the bed, and pulled me close to him.

"You good?"

"Not really, I feel so bad for Eva. She lost her mother and not even gone know it. Then, her grandmother is a real bitch. Do you know she told the detectives that she didn't care what they did with her body because she didn't have any money to bury her."

"Wow! That shit is foul. We can handle her funeral if you want to."

"Ky already told the detective that she and Brodie would handle it."

"Alright, well I'll shoot Bro a couple of dollars to go towards it. Now what's gone happen to little mama since the grandmom ain't worth shit."

"I don't know. I hope they don't put her in the system."

"Maybe Bro and Ky should take her. I mean, she already knows who they are." What Reem just said was a great idea, but right now, no one is thinking about that.

"I'll mention it after the funeral arrangements. Have you saw Taji, did he find Deja?"

"I just stopped by the studio before I came here, and no he hasn't seen her. That nigga pissed too, because she keeps sending him to voice mail."

"She just needs some space right now. I know exactly how she is feeling. As soon as Ky told me, the first thing came to mind was that could have been me years ago."

"Come on baby, don't think like that."

"It's true, Reem. What if you hadn't come when you did? I would have been dead and my babies wouldn't have a mother."

"Yeah, but you're here and the twins have a great mother. I'm sorry what happened to Rayne, Bailey, I am. But I don't want you starting with the what if's."

"You know what, Reem?"

"Yes baby, what's up?"

"Once Deja, get straight and is ready to leave the center, I think it's time for me to start staying home with you and the boys more. I'll still go in the center a couple of days of the week, but the majority of the time I'll be home. Ky and I can hire some people, or may Deja can run the center sometimes. She's already started school up, and I think she's doing the social worker thing."

"That's good. Then she will already have a job lined up when she leaves the center. Even though Taji ready to be in big money, and she ain't gone have to work."

"Since when does that matter. You've always been into big money, but I've always worked."

"Yeah you right, and that's why you always had my heart because you are a go-getter, and I ain't never had to worry about you being needy. Remember I wanted to buy you a house before we even started out and you weren't beat?"

"Yeah and ya slick ass gone buy the house anyway, and keep it hidden until we made it official."

"Yeah and ya ungrateful ass still didn't want it." I looked at Reem with my lip poked out.

"I'm not ungrateful, Tyreem."

"Wooh, I'm Tyreem now? You feel some type of way because I called you ungrateful; I was just playing, baby girl. Relax."

"I'm relaxed, to be honest, I'm tired as shit. The twins worked me over after work. They're getting so big and more active. Do you think they are too much for us to have another baby right now?" Reem gave me the side eye.

"Ummmmm, nah we will be fine. We do have a nanny and you just said you were cutting days down at work. Is there a reason why you're asking me about another baby?"

"Not really, I know we've talked about me wanting more kids, and you always agree with whatever I want. You never get into details about what Reem wants."

"We've been together for years B, you know I want kids, ma."

"Yeah I know that, but how many?"

"However many you wanna give me."

"See, here you go. It's always what I want."

"The reason why I feel that way is because it's your body, baby. I might tell you I want four kids and you might only want one more. It's your body. Who am I to make you have four kids if you want one? So, it's whatever you want. If you want one more, I'll give you one more. If you want ten more, I'll give you ten more. What's it gone be, one or ten?"

"I think I'll pass on the ten, maybe two more," I said while laughing at Reem's crazy ass.

"Now is there something you want to tell me? All this damn baby talk."

"Reem, I told you it wasn't nothing, I just wanted to know."

"Well since it ain't nothing, how about we try to make it something?" Reem said while putting me on top of him and kissing my lips passionately. My future husband and I explored each other's bodies for the rest of the night, but what Reem didn't know was that my period was late.

SAMAAD

It was now the next day and no one still has heard from Deja, and Tiombe was all fucked up over it. She was walking around the house slamming shit around with her lips all poked out.

"Come here, baby," I demanded. She walked over to me in slow motion for some reason. She must have sensed that I wasn't feeling her little attitude, because she started explaining as soon as she sat on my lap.

"I'm sorry I'm being so evil today, but I'm scared something happened to Deja. Maady, nobody has seen her all night. Shouldn't we file a missing person's report?"

"Usually it's twenty-four to forty-eight hours. Just give it a little more time, baby." Yeah we all were fucked up over what happened to Rayne, but of course, Deja took it harder than anyone else.

"Ok, well can we go riding around looking for her today?"

"Whatever you wanna do beautiful, is fine with me."

"I love you, Samaad."

"I love you too, baby." I was shocked I said that shit, but I couldn't deny my feelings. A nigga's head was gone over Tiombe, and to be honest, I've always been feeling her. But she wasn't ready.

"You know what else I wanna do while we out looking for Deja?"

"What else you wanna do?"

"I wanna stop by my mama's house. I think it's time you meet her."

"Where're your pops at?"

"I don't know, he left us when I was little. That's where all my man problems come from, I guess."

"Well, if that's the case, what made you come to my doorstep?"

"I told you that night I saw you brought back old feelings that I didn't even know I had. I'm not on no bullshit Maady, I'm ready to be somebody's wife and mother one day. All that clubbing, hanging out, and hopping in and out of beds wasn't gone get me that. When we were fucking around, I was feeling you then, I really was. But I didn't have all that hoe shit out of me. Hate to sound like that, but it's true."

Did her crazy ass just call herself a hoe? I couldn't do shit but laugh. Tiombe was as real as they come, and I loved every bit of it.

"Appreciate you for being real, and I believe you. That day you came here I was happy as hell to see ya ass, and I'm glad we finally made it official."

"If I ain't anything else, Imma always be real, baby," Tee said before she kissed me on my lips.

While we were kissing each other, I slid my hand up her shirt and started playing with her nipples. She let out a soft moan, letting me know she was enjoying the feeling. I lifted up so I could lay her on the bed. As soon as I stood up, she wrapped her legs around my waist. We were sitting on a chair that was in my room so we weren't far from the bed. Once I made it to the bed, I laid her on her back. She gave me an intense stare while I stripped out of my clothes. When I was completely naked, I then slid off Tee's little pajama shorts she had on with no panties underneath. My mouth watered looking at her pretty pussy.

"Do you want me to taste it?"

"No, I just want you to fuck the shit out of me right now. None of that foreplay shit, just give me the dick." She didn't have to tell me twice.

"Turn over and put that ass in the air," I barked. Tee smiled and did as she was told. Before I slid inside of her, I gave her two hard smacks to each ass cheek.

"Mmmm, hmmm, that's the way I like it, Maady."

I drilled in and out of her just the way she liked it. Her pussy was making all type of noises and that was all you could hear throughout the room, besides her moans. I was in a zone and the shit was feeling really good. While I was continuing to give her these long, hard strokes, she was going crazy as shit.

"Play with your pussy, Ma," I told her to pleasure herself while I was dicking her down. I slid my finger in her ass while she was rubbing her clit. That shit not only made her go wild, that shit had a nigga ready to nut instantly.

"Ohhhhhhhh Maady, baby that shit feels so good. I think I'm about to cum."

"This shit feels good to you, doesn't it? You wanna cum with me?"

"Yesssssssssssssssssss, Maady, I'm ready to cum with you. I'm cummin baby, I'm cummin baby," Tee yelled right before she came all over my dick. Then I came shortly after her, shooting all my seeds up in her ass. I meant to pull out but that shit was feeling too damn good.

"Man fuck, are you on any birth control?"

"You picked a nice time to ask that question and yes, I'm on birth control."

"My bad, I didn't mean for it to come out like that."

"You cool Maady, I understand, and trust me we too early in our relationship to be having kids."

"How many kids do you want, Tee?"

"My mom only had me, so I want a big family. Maybe four or five. What about you?"

"About four, but I want them all by the same woman. So, therefore, I want her to be my wife."

"I can understand that. You really wanna get married? Not too many street niggas be worried about marriage."

"Hell yeah I wanna get married."

"I wanna get married one day too," Tee said while yarning.

"I tired ya little ass out, didn't I?"

"Yup, and that's why Imma take this nap before we hit the streets."

"I guess we can take this nap together."

She cuddled up close to me, I kissed her forehead, and we both drifted off to sleep.

JACE

Deja's mom hasn't been answering when I called. So, I knew her ole ugly ass knew where the fuck her daughter was. She has just been holding out. The whole time Deja and I were together, she probably talked to me more than her own damn daughter. Now she is giving me her ass to kiss. Yeah, something is up. While I was pulling up the street, I saw a car pulling into the driveway, but it wasn't familiar. I hurried and parked my car where no one couldn't see me and then jumped out. I stood to the side where no one could see me, and to my surprise, Deja jumped out of the car. I was so excited, but I didn't wanna scare her off and I didn't want her to run in the house. I watched as she banged and banged on the door. A smile crept up on my face when I noticed no one was answering. Deja was so pissed she sat on the step, playing on her phone. When I noticed that she wasn't moving, I jumped back in my car and pulled up in front of the house. Then I jumped out of the car.

"Hey pretty lady, can I talk to you for a minute?" I asked. I could tell by the look on her face that she was in shock and didn't think that she was gone see me. She hesitated before she spoke.

"Hey Jace, how are you?"

"I'm good and you?"

"I'm ok."

"Come take a ride with me, Deja," I said while standing in front of her.

"No, Imma stay here and wait for my mama to come."

"Deja get the fuck up and get in the car," I said while now pointing my gun at her. She got up with tears running down her face, but she did as she was told.

"Jace, please don't hurt me."

"Baby, I'm not gone hurt you. I miss you so much," I assured her while getting in the car. Once she was in, I made sure to put the gun on my lap, in case she tried some funny shit. Deja didn't know it yet but I was never losing her again.

* * *

The ride to our house was quiet as hell. I hadn't been here in a minute, but I did have a cleaning crew clean it up for me. I also came by every now in then to check on it.

"Alright, come on Deja, we home now."

"Jace, I don't wanna go in that house. It is not my home."

"Deja, don't make me fuck you up! I don't know where you've been, but you know how I feel about that mouth of yours."

She didn't say anything else, she got out the car and headed for the door. Once we made it in the house, she stood by the door like she was a stranger. She had me ready to beat her ass already, but I was trynna chill. I walked over to her and grabbed her arm and pulled her over to the couch.

"Why, are you always so rough with me?" Deja asked.

"I'm not trying to be, but you are pissing me the fuck off." I barked.

"I'm not talking about now. I'm talking about all the time. I wanna know everything. I wanna know why did you beat me every chance you got?" Hearing her throw question after question at me had me shocked. She was different, this wasn't the old Deja.

"Most of the time, you didn't listen, that's why."

"Jace, I'm not ya fucking property. So, you thought putting your hands on me and making me stay in the house was normal?"

"Look Deja, I don't know where all these questions are coming from, but this is not how I wanna spend our day back together."

"Jace I'm telling you now, I ain't staying here."

I had just about enough. I walked over to her and slapped the shit out of her. She felt her face and licked the blood and slapped my ass the hell back right across my face.

"What the fuck, Deja!" Her hitting me back had me fucked up. As long as I've known Deja, she has never hit me back. She looked up at me with this crazy look on her face, then she laughed at me.

"See, when I hit you. You didn't like that shit, did you?" I grabbed a handful of her hair and dragged her upstairs to the room.

"I wasn't gone do this to you, but since you wanna be all tough and shit, I'm about to handcuff ya stupid ass to the bed."

"No please Jace, I'm sorry. Don't do this, please."

"Shut up and stop that damn crying and maybe I'll let you loose tonight, and we can watch movies together."

Once I locked her up, I went to the bathroom to shower. Deja had my mind all fucked up. I couldn't believe she had just hit me back. Something must have happened to her, because this was not her. I turned the water on to the temperature I liked, then jumped in. Still shocked and confused about what just went down, I stayed in a while just letting the water run on me. Feeling ready to get the hell out of the shower, I washed and rinsed my body then jumped out. I dried my body, wrapped the towel around my waist, then walked in my bedroom. I must have been in the shower for a while, because Deja had fallen to sleep. I walked over to her and kissed her forehead. Her cheeks were still wet from her crying. Not wanting to bother her, I slipped some ballers on and a wife beater and headed downstairs to watch TV.

KYLAYDA

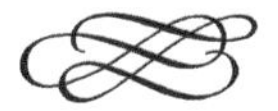

It was about two in the morning and Eva woke up screaming, "Mommy". I guess she was starting to realize that Rayne hadn't been around. I found myself sitting in the rocking chair, rocking her back to sleep, crying my heart out. This was going to be a hard transition for her. Even though she doesn't really know what death was, she did know something was wrong because she didn't see her mommy anymore. After rocking her back to sleep, I went downstairs to get something to drink. I doubt if I would be able to go right back to sleep after this. Once I made it to my kitchen, I grabbed my water out of the fridge, then I sat at the table.

"Baby, what's wrong? You good?"

"Yeah, I'm ok Papi, you can go ahead and go back to sleep."

"Now you know I can't sleep without you lying next to me. How's princess doing? I heard her crying."

"She woke up screaming for Rayne. So, I had to rock her back to sleep."

"Let me guess, you cried the whole time you rocked her back to sleep. Now you're in your feelings and can't go back to sleep."

"You know ya wife so well." Brodie walked over to the table and sat down with me.

"So, when we gone go talk to Rayne's mother?"

"I didn't know you wanted to come."

"Yeah, I wanna come. I need to know what's up with the princess, too. Like, is there any family that she can live with?"

"That's been on my mind as well. I know she doesn't want Eva, so where will she go?"

"If she doesn't want her, she can just give her to us."

"You really wouldn't mind her living with us, Brodie?"

"Ky, I told you we could adopt kids since we can't have any of our own."

A smile crept up on my face and I was ecstatic right now. I swear I loved this man with all my heart.

"Well you know we would have to handle this the legal way. If we are gone to adopt her I want the paperwork stamped and sealed. I don't want no one to come later on down the line and think they can just take our baby back."

"We gone do everything the right way so that she can be ours. You don't have to worry about none of that."

"I love you so much, Papi."

"I love you too, baby. Now come on to bed so I can rub ya bootie and put ya ass back to sleep."

I got up from the table and followed my husband back up to our room. The talk we had put me in a better mood a little bit. I still was upset about Rayne, but it was nothing I could do. One thing is for sure, I will be the best mommy I can be to Eva.

* * *

The sun shining in my face woke me up out of my sleep. I looked over on Brodie's side of the bed and he was already up. I got up and went the bathroom to wash my face and brush my teeth before I went to get Eva ready for breakfast. Once I was finished in the bathroom, I went to the room where Eva was sleeping and she wasn't in there. I assumed she was downstairs with Brodie. Heading downstairs, the front door opened and Eva and Brodie were walking in.

"Good morning, beautiful."

"Hey baby, where y'all two coming from?"

"Well, little princess here came in the room smacking me in my face this morning, hollering eat, so I got up to get her something to eat. I didn't want any damn cereal and you were sleeping so peaceful and I didn't wanna wake you. So, we went and ate at the Waffle House and we brought you some food back."

"Hey, my Eva," I said while holding my arms out to pick her up. She came right to me and I walked in the kitchen to sit at the table to eat my food.

"We need to get her a highchair, and some other things. I'm chilling with y'all two all day, so we can do some shopping for her after we come from seeing her grandmom."

"Brodie, what if we buy her a bunch of stuff and she ends up not staying with us?"

"Then she'll take it all wherever she goes."

I wasn't gone to argue with him he had his mind made up already. I ate my food then went upstairs to dress Eva and I. I looked her up and down and couldn't believe that Brodie took her out of this house in her pajamas.

An hour went by and Eva and I were now dressed. When we made it downstairs, Brodie smiled at us like he was the happiest man in the world. I hope everything with Eva works out, because my husband was getting too attached to her. From the first moment he saw her, she went right to him as if she knew him from somewhere. So, now they have a little bond; Rayne used to let us take her to the park and everything.

"Why are you looking at us like that?" I sassed.

"You both are so beautiful," Brodie said then winked at me.

"Well thank you Papi, you don't look too bad yourself."

"Y'all ready to go?"

"I'm not, but this has to be done right away."

The last thing I wanted to do was talk to Rayne's mother, but we needed to discuss a couple of things. Rayne's funeral arrangements were first on the list. I needed answers from this old bag. Who the fuck tells the detective to do whatever he wants with their child's body?

"Baby, you don't have to worry about anything. I'll be right by your side, and if you feel like you getting too upset to talk, I'll take over."

After Bro assured me that everything would be ok, we headed to the car, and were on our way. It took us about a half hour to get to Rayne's mom's house. There was a car parked in her driveway, so we assumed she was home. Brodie parked the car and walked around to the passenger side door, then opened it for me. Then he opened the back door and got Eva out of her car seat.

"Hey little mama, you ready to go," Brodie asked Eva while smiling. She'd already stolen his heart in such a little time. Eva nodded her head yes then kissed Brodie's cheek.

"Awwwww, now wasn't that cute," I beamed. We locked the car up, then headed up to the door. Brodie had Eva in his arms so I walked ahead of them to knock on the door. As soon as I was about to knock again, her evil looking ass opened the door.

"What the hell you knocking on my damn door like that for?"

Hello Ms. King, I'm here to talk to you about Rayne's funeral arrangements."

"Imma tell you the same thing I told that detective, I don't have no money to be giving nobody no damn funeral."

"Listen ma'am, watch how you talk to my wife. We wanted to let you know that we were paying for everything. I just need to know if she has a lot of family. If not, we will make this a small private service. If you have a big family, we will do it big. After you tell us what we need to know, trust and believe we won't need you for anything else. Now can we go in and talk?" Brodie barked. My husband knew I was getting annoyed so he took over.

"Come on in," Ms. King retorted. I could tell she had an attitude, but she wasn't gone try Brodie. We all walked to the living room and sat on the couch. The look in Eva's eyes told us she didn't wanna be here.

"So would you prefer Rayne to have a big service or small?"

"We don't have much family and her daddy never did shit for her, so I doubt if he would come anyway. So, a small private service is fine. If y'all don't mind me asking, why y'all doing all this for a girl you barely knew?"

"First and foremost, no cursing in front of Eva, and secondly your daughter was so sweet and had a kind heart. She did not deserve the life she was given, and in such a little time I'd learned to love her. Now another thing we need to know, what will happen to Eva now that her mother is no longer here."

"They called and told me that she would come to me, but I don't want no babies. I raised Rayne and I don't wanna raise her daughter."

"Well I'll take Eva if you don't want her. Imma just need you to come with me and we can get this all situated the right way."

"Ok, just let me know when you are ready. I would like to see Eva sometimes as well." I didn't know about that but she was her grand-mother, so I would want Eva to know her.

"That's fine with us, but we would have to sit with you while Eva visits. I can see she don't feel comfortable around you. We also don't want any problems with you. Once she's with us, she's with us. Ain't no you want her back," Brodie fussed.

"She looks happy with you two. I can tell the way she won't let go. I haven't been the best mother to Rayne, so I know I wouldn't be any good for Eva. Just do me a favor and be the best parents y'all can be to my grandbaby."

After we talked to her a little more we left and headed to Willie Watkins to make arrangements for Rayne's service.

DEJA

Waking up to Jace's head in between my legs annoyed me, but I knew I had to be nice. I needed to regain his trust so he can feel comfortable with letting me roam the house again.

"Ohhhhhh shit Jace, that feels so damn good, baby," a fake moan escaped my lips.

I was acting like I was enjoying the moment, but I wanted to kick his ass right in the face. If I weren't making any reaction, he would know I wasn't into it. No matter how much I didn't wanna do this, I had to, so what I was gone do was pretend he was Taji eating my pussy. He started flicking his tongue on my clit in a fast motion that drove my body wild. Picturing Taji in my head, I ended up bussing my first nut I had in a while. Jace got up and looked me in my face and smiled.

"I see I still got it, so are you ready for this dick?"

"Yes, I'm ready for it. But can you unlock me, please?"

"I'll unlock you. But if you try some funny shit Deja, I swear Imma fuck you up."

"Come on Jace, don't ruin the mood. I told you I'm ready for that dick."

Jace unlocked my hands and I turned around and put my ass in the air, giving him all access to hit it from the back. I didn't wanna look his ass in the face, and I didn't wanna fuck up my thoughts of Taji.

"Mmm, Hmm. I'm about to tear that ass up," Jace said. He tried just sticking his dick straight inside, but I was tight as hell. He had to take his time.

"Fuck Jace, that shit hurt. Slow down baby, it's been a minute."

He eased his way in inch by inch until he was all the way in. Once he was in, he started giving me the business and I still wasn't pressed.

"Damn Ma, this shit tight and wet just like I remember. Shit, I miss this pussy so much."

I hated hearing his annoying ass talk. I wanted his ass the buss a nut real quick and get the fuck away from me. So, I started talking shit all kinds of shit.

"Yessssss, Jace, just like that baby. Show me how much you miss me."

The more shit I talked, the faster he started moving in and out of me. I started tightening up my pussy muscles on his dick to help this process speed up.

"FUCK! Deja I'm cummin, Ma," Jace yelled. *Go ahead motherfucker, hurry up,* I said to myself. As soon as he bust his nut he pulled me close to him. Y'all don't know how much I just felt like vomiting.

"Deja, I love you so much and I swear I'm gone try to do better," Jace said while dozing off. One of his favorite lines I didn't miss at all. I was gone let him sleep for a little while, then I was gone to get up. After about a half hour, I figured he was good and sleep, so I went to get up.

"Deja, don't play with me lay ya ass down," Jace barked.

I swear his stupid ass was sleep. I had to get the fuck out of here. He was not keeping me prisoner somewhere I didn't wanna be. All my friends were probably worried about me. I laid back down like he said and he had a fucking death grip on my ass. My phone was all the way on the other side of the room in my pocket. I knew it was dead because it wasn't going off. I should have listened to everyone and stayed my ass in the center. What happened to Rayne had me all fucked up, and I needed to get out, not knowing I was gone run into this fool. I knew it was a matter of time and I was gone see him again. After he slapped me last night I knew and I hit him back, I knew I wasn't gone deal with him hitting me again. I was getting the fuck out of this house between today and tomorrow.

* * *

"Deja, wake up baby so you can take a shower. I ordered some Chinese. I know you're hungry."

"Come now Taji, baby lets me get some sleep."

Whap, Whap, Whap

"What the fuck did you just call me?" Jace barked, delivering slap after slap to my face. My ass was good and woke now.

"Jace, why the fuck you hit me like that? I didn't do shit to you," I screamed.

"Deja, don't fucking play with me. You just called me Taji. Were you fucking him? Is that your new man?"

"Jace. I didn't call you no fucking Taji." I was now scared shitless and crying my heart out. Yeah I talked back and cursed at him, but the look in his eyes scared the shit out of me. It's like his shit went black, and he was ready to kill me.

"Yes the fuck you did. Where the fuck is your phone at?"

"I don't know." He grabbed my hair and pulled it hard as hell.

"Deja don't fucking play with me. Where the fuck is your phone?"

"Jace you're hurting me, let go of my hair."

"I'm not letting shit go until you tell me what the fuck I wanna know." He gripped my hair tighter. The shit was beginning to give me a headache.

"My phone is in my pants pocket."

Jace let my hair go and went to grab my phone. When he picked it up, I could see he was annoyed. He walked out of the room, then came back with a phone charger. It didn't come right on because of it being dead for a minute.

"So, Imma ask you this one more time. Are you fucking that corny ass nigga?"

"I told you no Jace, you are still the only man I've ever had sex with."

"Well what do you and that nigga have going on for you to call me his name. You were fucking dreaming about that nigga, Deja. You ain't gone tell me y'all ain't got shit going on."

While he was giving me the death stare, my phone started going off like crazy. As soon as he picked it up, he sat back on the bed and went the everything. His face was red as shit and he was angry. I knew when he finished this might just be the end of my life.

TAJI

We were all chilling in Reem's crib trying to figure out how we were going to find Deja. It had been going on the second day since we'd seen her.

"Man, where the hell could she be?"

"Maybe she went home?" Reem said.

"No, she wouldn't have gone home to him," Tee assured us.

"How do you know what she would have done? She used to shut you out when she was with that nigga," Reem said.

"Because I know my best friend and I ain't gone let y'all sit here and make her out to be some dummy for going back to his bitch ass," Tee fussed.

"Look baby girl, ain't nobody says she was a dummy. The fact of the matter is these women need help, and they have to be ready for it. When they're not, sometimes the go back. I've grown to love Deja and I want her back here safe like everybody else," Reem barked.

"Alright, everybody calms down. We all are in our feelings right now. We haven't even had time to grieve over Rayne and now Deja is missing. What we won't do is be at each other's throat," Bailey fumed. My phone going off brought me out of my thoughts.

Deja: *I'm good I decided to go back home with Jace.*

Me: *Deja are you serious you know what just happened to Rayne*

Deja: *I'll be good Taji*

Me: *Alright Ma I'll erase your number have a nice life*

Deja: *I'm sorry for wasting your time.*

"That nigga got her and if he hurts her I'm killing his ass on the spot," I said while handing Reem my phone and walking out of the door; I needed some air. Deja did not go back to that nigga, I know in my heart she didn't do that to me.

"I'm sorry, cuz. I told you don't put ya all into it because she might not have been ready."

"Reem, I know in my heart she didn't get back to that nigga. I'm just not believing that shit."

"She sent Bailey and Ky a text to tell them she was sorry for wasting their time. They sent her the information for Rayne's service and told her she's welcome back anytime. She even called her home-girl and told her that she was with Jace and she was safe. Tee cursed her ass out then hung the phone up."

Hearing everything that Reem just told me had me fucked up. I need to go and grab me a drink. Reem handed me my phone and I took off, making sure to stop by the liquor store first. Then, I was going to my studio. When I tell y'all my heart was crushed, I didn't know what to do with myself. While I was driving I felt my phone going off. I answered without seeing who it was.

"What! I yelled on the phone.

"Well damn I'm sorry to bother you," Kaci replied

"I'm sorry Kaci, going through some shit today."

"I just wanted to know were you at the studio."

"I'm actually on my way after I hit the liquor store."

"You already have a bottle of Henny at the studio."

"Oh shit I forgot about that. Thanks baby girl, I'll be there in like ten minutes."

Yes, my ass been drinking since last night. This shit ain't even me. No female has ever affected me. I hope to God she's ok for Jace's sake. I swear on my family, I'm going to end up killing this nigga. Rayne's funeral is in two days. If she doesn't come, I know something is wrong. I really wanna go over there right now, but Imma chill because the truth is, Reem could be right. Of course, I don't want him to be right, but this shit is real.

Twenty minutes went by and I was pulling up to the studio. Kaci was also pulling up. She got out of the car and she had on a crop top, some baggy jeans, and a pair of Jordan 12's. Her hair was bone straight with a part down the middle. I swear she was different. She had her own style that made her stand out. Not to mention she was beautiful. The only thing stopping me was the feelings I have for Deja and I didn't wanna mix business with pleasure. Shit, if I could fuck without feelings getting involved I certainly would because a nigga needed to relieve some stress bad as hell.

"Hey Taji, what's good?"

"I'm good Kaci, how about you, and I'm sorry for snapping when I answered the phone."

"It's cool. I've noticed since last night that something was going on with you."

"Come on, let's go inside." I opened the studio and we headed to one of the rooms.

"So, I've been working on something new, and I wanted you to hear it."

"Alright, well let me hear it."

Never really knowing how to tell you I'm feeling you

It's just something about the way you walk, the way you talk

Baby can we try to see where these feelings go

"You wrote this yourself, Kaci?"

"Yes, I was just chilling and pulled out my book and got to writing."

"Girl, you got a gift. You can sing and write. You gone be a great asset to Price Records."

"So, that means you like it?"

"Yeah man, I love it."

"Tell me what's going on. You don't have to tell me if you don't want to, but sometimes talking helps."

"Somebody that I'm feeling is in a fucked up situation, and I'm trying my hardest to hang around and wait until she's ready. Everybody is telling me to not put my all into it because she might not be ready. The way I'm feeling about her keeps me from talking to anyone different. Like, am I crazy for waiting around? What if we end up not being together?"

"What if you end up letting her go, and then the next nigga end up being with her. I'm a firm believer in if it's meant to be, it'll happen. I say follow your heart. One thing is for sure, she's a lucky girl, and Imma chill on my thoughts," Kaci chuckled.

"You was checking for a nigga?"

"Yup, I sure was. So if lil mama doesn't work out, I'll be right here waiting."

"I wouldn't mix business with pleasure, but no offense, you bad as hell and I'm attracted to you. I just wouldn't wanna mess up our work relationship together. I just want us to make some great hits and some even better money. You down with that?"

"I'm always down for money and music. So, let's get to recording."

Kaci and I stayed in the studio recording her song. Between this song and the one she let me hear the other night, she had an alright start for her album. Plus, working was the only thing that kept my mind off Deja.

TYREEM

Everybody had an attitude lately because of the Deja situation. I knew my cousin was mad at what I said, but I needed him to know that he had to be prepared for something like this to happen. I did apologize to Tee because I didn't want her thinking I was straight up disrespectful. Bailey comes home and tells me plenty of stories, and a lot of these chicks go back home to that man who hurts them. Some of them are scared to death and others' heads are just messed up. After they all left, I cleaned the kitchen and let Bailey rest for the night. I even bathed the boys and put them to bed. Now I was sitting and watching TV until I got tired.

"What you doing down here?"

"Watching TV, I didn't wanna wake you."

"I can't sleep, I'm up thinking about Deja."

"Well talk to me about it. Do you think she went back to that nigga, or do you think she's in harm?"

"She was in harm the minute she ended up back with him. Deja is different from Rayne, though. She would have called us herself and let us know she was staying with him. Shit, we already know he's abusive. When I first met Deja, she told Ky and I that she didn't know if she was over him, but she was gone damn sure try to get over him. She's been straightforward with us ever since she came. If she wanted to be back with him, I truly believe that she would have called and told us rather then send everybody a text message."

"She called Tee, though."

"That's because he knows Tee and he probably wasn't expecting her to be with us. I just hope if she's there against her will she finds a way out. We taught her plenty of survival tactics when she first came."

Bailey had a point, but it could also be a chance that she did go back to him. I was gone keep my thoughts to myself. I didn't wanna get my girl upset.

"Well just keep in touch with her by texting and trying to call, and Rayne's funeral is in a couple of days. If she doesn't make it, we will take the whole crew over that bitch and make sure she's good."

"Alright baby, we can do that. I'm going back to bed and I'll send her a text. Are you coming to bed now?"

"I guess, if you want me to. I have to get up early in the morning anyway."

"What you mean if I want you to, Tyreem?" When she calls me Tyreem I know she's feeling some type of way. I laughed at her and jumped up, then ran over to her and pulled her in for a hug.

"I was only joking and here you go with that Tyreem shit."

"What, that's your name ain't it?"

"Yeah, but that's not what you call me. Every time you call me that, I know you are feeling some type away or you about to curse my ass out," Bailey and I headed upstairs and climbed into our bed.

"I love you Tyreem," Bailey chuckled.

"I love you too, baby. Now take ya crazy ass to sleep."

* * *

"Daddy, daddy, daddy, daddy," the twins screamed and jumped on the bed, waking me up.

"Boys, quit jumping on my bed before I beat y'all."

"You better not beat my kids, Bailey," I said jumping up.

"Well make they badasses sit down, Reem."

"Come on y'all, let's go get some cereal." I grabbed Braylon and Braxton, then headed downstairs.

"Why y'all up there jumping on the bed acting up?"

"Dat was him," Braylon said pointing to his brother.

"So, you just gone lie like I didn't see you jumping too?" I chuckled and poured them both some cereal. These boys were my life and they knew they had me. I would never let Bailey hit them. You couldn't tell me I didn't birth them. They were mine even though they didn't come from me.

"Hurry up boys and eat so that we can go."

"They going in with you today?"

"Yeah, I gave the nanny the week off. I told Ky I was gone start letting them attend the daycare at the center."

"That's good so that they can interact with other kids. They gone be going to regular school soon."

"I know right, they getting so damn big so fast."

"They moving out of the way for that other baby that's coming soon."

"Well, I hope I'm Mrs. Price before that happens."

"Hurry up and get those wedding plans handled. If it was up to me, you could be Mrs. Price today. I don't need a big ass wedding like you ladies like."

"You told me I could have the wedding of my dreams and that's what I want," Bailey sassed. I held my hands up in the air like I was surrendering.

"It's ya call baby girl, whatever you want."

"Where's Taji at? It feels like I hadn't seen him since early yesterday."

"Oh he hit me last night and told me he was staying in the studio all night. He is working on some shit."

"Alright, I hope he is ok. He left yesterday in his feelings."

"He's a little fucked up, but he's a Price, he'll get over it soon." One thing about the men in my family, when we are going through some shit, we bury ourselves in work.

"I hope Deja finds her way back to him. I can tell they love each other. Taji just has to be patient with her, and Deja just has to let her guard down for the right man. It's going to be hard but love conquers all. It's rough loving a damaged woman, and make sure you talk to him about it, baby. You know off-hand how hard it is, and we've made it through some hard situations. I love you even more for all you did to stay with me. It was rough, but you weren't letting me go."

"That was never happening, baby. You and the boys are my everything. I was gone do whatever it took to get y'all in my life and to keep y'all happy. Now get out before you be late for work in here talking all this mushy shit."

Bailey burst out laughing and started cleaning up the boys so they can leave.

"I just want you to talk to Taji, and don't hold nothing back. I know you've talked to him, but I know you didn't tell him everything. You're so secretive about when we first started out, so I know you didn't get into detail with him. I think he needs to know what comes with loving a woman like Deja."

"Alright baby, I'll talk to him today, I promise. Have a nice day at work and call me if you need me."

I kissed her and the boys' foreheads and walked them to the door. Once I made sure they were safe inside the car and she pulled off, I shut and locked the door, then headed upstairs to take care of my hygiene.

SAMAAD

Tee and I were having dinner at her mom's house and Deja's mom showed up. I knew Tee wasn't in the mood to talk about Deja, but I knew she would be the topic of the day.

"So, have you heard from Deja, Tee?" Ms. Denise asked.

"Yeah, she called me earlier. She told me to let you know she was fine."

"If she's fine, why hasn't she been answering anyone."

"Mama D, she's fine. Now, can we please stop talking about her," Tee snapped.

"She went back to him, didn't she, Samaad?" Deja's mom asked me.

"Yes, she sent us all messages telling us she is fine, and she called Tee."

"It's nothing no one can do, Ma'am. Deja has to want to leave him. If she doesn't press charges and get away, the cops won't even help. This has been a crazy week for Tee and I. We have been going through it, that's why she snapped."

"Tee baby, I love this young man. What took you so long to bring him home to meet me?" Ms. Tina asked.

"There goes that smile I love so much," I smirked at Tee.

Tee's mom hopped up, went to the stove, and started bringing all the food to the table. Ms. Denise looked like she was sad and upset. I knew the shit with Deja was fucking with her bad. Shit, we all in our feelings about it, and we hope she gets out before it's too late. After like three trips from the stove to the table, a big ass spread of everything was sitting on the table. I don't know why she cooked all this food for four people. We ain't even gone eat half of this food.

"Mama, why you cook all this food? It's only four of us here."

"I wanted to make sure I had a little of everything, because I wasn't sure what Samaad ate."

"I appreciate all this food you cooked, too."

"Your welcome baby. Now say grace Tee." Everyone put their heads down, while Tee said grace. When she was done, we all started passing around trays and making our plates.

"So Mr. Samaad, tell me a little about your family."

"Well I'm an only child, and it's just my mama and me. I never met my daddy, and my mama is my world."

"What are your intentions with my baby."

"I plan on loving and treating her like the queen she is."

"Is marriage in your future?"

"Mama, why are you asking him all those questions?"

"It's cool, baby. She just feeling me out, trynna make sure I'm right for you."

"Honestly ma'am yes, marriage is in my future. I love ya daughter and I plan on being around for a while. So get used to seeing my face, mama," I assured Tee's mom.

"Tina, leave that boy alone before you run him out of here," Ms. Denise fussed.

"Denise, shut up and mind ya damn business. I'm just trynna make sure he ain't trynna play my baby."

"Nah, Ms. Tina, I'm too grown to be playing games."

"Alright mama, that's enough, let's just eat our food, please."

The room got quiet and we all just ate our food. I looked around the table and saw that Ms. Denise was in deep thought, just playing in her food with her fork. I hoped nothing happened to Deja. After we finished dinner, we were heading home.

"Baby, can we go by Deja's house? I just wanna see for myself that she is doing well."

"Of all nights, when I ain't strapped, you wanna go to Jace's house."

"Don't worry, baby mama stay strapped."

I don't even know why I was shocked hearing her say that. Tiombe was really about that life.

"What you doing strapped, Tee?"

"One night I was leaving the club, and I was almost raped. So the very next day, I went to a shooting range, bought me a gun, and learned how to shoot. I ain't got time for no big ass nigga twice my size to be taking advantage of me. Now if they try it, I have some hot shit for they asses."

All I could do was shake my head at her crazy little ass.

"Well, make sure you only use that bitch on outsiders," I chuckled.

"Oh baby, you good as long as you don't try me," Tee giggled.

"Don't play with me, Tiombe."

"Wooh, you said my whole name. Did I piss you off ?"

"No, not at all. I just needed you to know I mean what I said."

Fifteen minutes went by and we were now pulling up in front of Jace's crib. His car was there so we knew he was home I just hope he doesn't be on no bullshit.

JACE

Quan and Lola had been calling me like crazy, but I knew I couldn't leave Deja's sneaky ass in the house alone. After she explained everything about Taji and the crew, I was shocked I didn't beat her ass. I calmed myself down and made her promise that she wouldn't leave me again. I also threaten to kill her mama and Tee if she tried to leave me again. She agreed and we'd been chilling all day.

"Are you ready to eat, Jace?"

"Yes baby, you can make my plate."

It felt so good having Deja back home. She had my house clean, and I had me a home-cooked meal. She walked my plate in the living room to me, then she went back to get hers. I watched her sexy ass walk back into the kitchen. Deja was wearing some little ass pajama shorts and a wife beater with no panties or bra on. She had me ready to bend her ass over the couch, but I would wait until later to handle her ass. My phone was going off once again and I looked to see who it was, and it was Quan again. I guess this nigga really needed some money. Deja came back with her plate and we sat and ate together.

"I miss these days together."

"Well Jace you could have these days you just need to stop hitting on me."

"I know Deja and Imma do better baby."

"Can I get my phone after dinner to call mama to see how she's doing?"

"You can use my phone to call her."

"Jace, she not gone answer from your phone. You gone be sitting right here when I call, why can't I just use my phone?"

"Alright Deja, but don't try no funny shit."

"Or what Jace, you are gone beat my ass? See what I mean, you just told me you were gone do better not even five minutes ago."

Man I swear her slick ass mouth was killing me these days. She just wouldn't shut the fuck up. I just didn't say anything. As long as I was quiet she was quiet. If I said something else and she got smart, I was gone fuck her up. When Deja finished eating, she grabbed my plate and hers, then headed to the kitchen to wash the dishes. A half hour passed and she was headed back into the living room. She came over to me and sat right on my lap.

"Can I call my mama now?" I handed her the phone, then tapped her so she could get up. I need to use the bathroom real quick.

"You better be calling ya mama and that's it," I said while I headed to the bathroom. After using the bathroom and walking back to the living I stood to the side to hear Deja's conversation.

"Mama, I'm good, you don't have to worry, and I'll be to see you soon." After that she had disconnected her call so I decided to go ahead in the living room.

"So Jace, did you make up your mind about the funeral?"

"Not yet, but I'll let you know early in the morning."

"Remember you can come with me, but I really don't wanna miss it."

"Alright, I told you I'd let you know."

I wasn't going to no fucking funeral for no bitch I didn't know, and Deja wasn't going either. She didn't know that damn girl. I wasn't gone tell her that just yet, I needed her to give me a great night. She thinks a nigga is slow. I see she trynna stay on my good side so I can let her ass go to that funeral. A knock at my door brought us out of our thoughts. I wasn't expecting any company, so I knew I had to give Deja a little pep talk.

"Listen, I don't know who this is. But if you try anything, I will kill your mama and Tee, and I mean it Deja." I jumped up and went to answer the door and it was Samaad and Tee.

"Hey, is Deja here?" Tee asked.

"She here, but I don't think I want you in my house."

"Jace don't be like that, let her in."

"Only because my girl wants you in here is the only reason you are coming in." I knew when I said that Tee didn't like it, but I didn't give a fuck.

"Yo man, don't be disrespecting my girl. Make it ya last fucking time if you don't want me to beat ya ass, my nigga," Samaad barked. When they walked in Deja ran to both of them and hugged them tightly. The shit pissed me off so fucking bad. I wanted they asses to leave and get the fuck out of my house, but I was gone hold my anger in for Deja.

"So what y'all been up to. I miss y'all so much."

"You don't have to miss us. You could be still with us."

"Come on Tee, don't start that shit," Samaad barked.

"So when did y'all become the happy couple?" I needed to ask because the last time me and Samaad hung together, he didn't have a girl.

"We've been going strong for a while now, but why you act as if you care?" Samaad said.

"Damn man, it's like that? You have been giving me ya ass to kiss for a minute now."

"Nigga, shit changed when you started putting ya hands on my little sis."

"Look Deja, baby I'm sorry but they gotta go. They only came over to see if you are still alive. She good, now y'all can get the fuck out. I ain't gone be disrespected in my own motherfucking house."

"Nigga we were about to leave anyway. It's hard to be in the same room with ya punk ass without wanting to fuck you up. As soon as Deja give me the word, I'm fucking you clean up. Believe that."

Samaad and his hoe ass girl both got up. After giving Deja hugs and kisses, they left out.

"They are not welcomed in my house no fucking more Deja, and I mean that shit."

"Alright Jace, but don't holler at me, I didn't invite them over her," Deja said and stormed off. I wanted to yank her by her hair and fuck her up, but I didn't I just let her go and sat my ass back down to watch TV. Once my shows were over, I would head up to bed. But right now, I need to calm my nerves down.

KYLAYDA

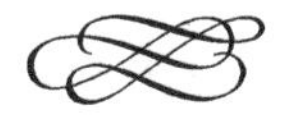

"Good morning, beautiful."

"Hey Papi, what are you doing up so early?"

"I couldn't sleep. What about you?"

"I couldn't, either. I still can't believe we are laying Rayne to rest today."

"Right. When we went to go see her body yesterday I couldn't hold back the tears. Seeing little mama lying there in a casket had me fucked up. What are you doing with Eva today?"

"Imma go ahead and take her to the daycare. Then pick her up when we headed home."

"Alright cool, because she doesn't need to see any of this."

"Brodie, do you think we are doing the right thing adopting Eva?"

"Of course, we doing the right thing. What's wrong, why are you having doubts?"

"I don't know. I guess the whole thought of being someone's mama has me a little shook, that's all.

"Ain't no need for all that, you'll be a great mom. Shit, you already a great mom to her, so stop doubting yourself."

"I know, baby, I just don't want to fail Eva."

"Eva will be fine and you know you're not doing it alone. Not to mention Bailey, Reem, and the rest of the crew. Speaking of the crew, have Deja been responding to your text messages?"

"Yeah, she text me back the other night, but it just didn't seem like it was her. Every text was short and simple. Never any conversation."

"Well today is the day, and if she doesn't make it to the funeral, Reem said we are going to Jace's crib to make sure she good."

"I can't wait until I know she's good. That shit is killing me not knowing."

"I know, baby. I think this shit is fucking with everybody. Who would have ever thought we all would have gotten this close to these young ladies? I mean the center has been open for years and I've never known us all to get close to any of the girls."

"It was something special about these two. The minute they walked in the center, they had Ky and me. Then when y'all met them at the engagement lunch, y'all clicked. Even Eva wanted to be all up on you," I chuckled.

"Don't be hating because my little princess fell in love with me as soon as she met me," Brodie laughed.

"She did, and now look how attached to you she is. Shit, she'd rather come to you before me."

"So what, don't be getting jealous. Eva loves you, too."

"I'm glad we can take her in and make her the happiest little girl in the world."

"I wouldn't have had it any other way. To be honest with you, I was thinking about asking Rayne could we be her godparents. Since Eva adapted to us so well."

"Really baby? I didn't know that. Eva stole ya heart."

We had been laying in bed talking for hours about nothing. Now it was time to get up and get ready for the funeral. We decided to have it in the funeral home since it was a small service. Rayne didn't have much family, but the little she did have would be in attendance.

"Well, I guess we should be getting up now and getting our day ready."

"Yeah we should, but I ain't ready for this."

"Come here, beautiful. I know today is gone be hard for you, but remember, I'll be there with you every step of the way. We need to be strong for Eva," Brodie said while pulling me closer to him.

"I love you, Mr. Monroe, you mean the world to me."

"I know, now come on and let's get ready. We have a little over an hour to get dressed then get Eva dressed. Then take her to the center, and then get the funeral home."

"Damn I didn't realize it was this damn late. I'll get dressed in Eva's bathroom. That way I can get her ready while I'm getting ready."

We both jumped up and started moving around fast as hell. Every time me and my husband have long talks, we get so caught up at the moment.

* * *

An hour and a half had passed and we were just now pulling up to the funeral home. It was a good thing I made sure everything was situated last night, because Brodie and I were late as hell. My eyes were puffy, so I made sure I had on my big black Channel shades, and my black hat. Of course, I had a long black dress to match, while my husband had on a black Tom Ford suit with a black shirt to match. We didn't dress up much, but when we did, we threw it on. I asked for everyone to be in black while I dressed Rayne in white. When I saw her yesterday, she didn't look like herself, but they made sure to do the best that they could. I had to get the prettiest scarf I could find to wrap around her neck to cover the handprints.

"You good, baby?" Brodie asked right before we walked in the door.

"Yes, I'm fine. Let's go pay our respects."

Once we entered, everyone was in attendance, except for Deja. But it wasn't over yet, I'm sure she would be there soon. If it was one thing I knew about Deja, I knew she wouldn't miss this for the world. The whole crew was sitting up front, and so was Rayne's mother and she looked really nice today. We wanted her to do the eulogy, but she said she couldn't talk, so Bailey decided to say a little something from the heart.

"Today, we are here to celebrate the life of Ms. Rayne King. We were asked to keep it short and simple today, and all cards you have for the family will be given to her mother. Rayne leaves behind her daughter Eva King and her mother, Robin King. She also leaves behind a host of family and friends. Now we will have her mentor, Ms. Bailey Monroe, come up to the front and tell us a little something about Ms Rayne."

After the funeral director got done with his little speech, Bailey walked up to the front.

"Good morning, everyone. Many of you don't know me, but my name is Bailey Monroe. I am Rayne's mentor and a really good friend of hers, and I would like to share some of my thoughts with you all. While I was preparing for this speech for y'all, I had no clue what to say. See, I haven't known Rayne for a long period, but that saying, *We don't meet people by accident, they are meant to cross our path for a reason.* Rayne was sent to my family for a reason. I don't know exactly what the reason is, but I know it was meant to happen.

"The impact that she had on our hearts in such a short time shows it all. Me and Rayne lived similar lives, and not everyone can relate to what we've been through. I'm going to miss our long talks, but I'm going to keep her memory alive for Eva. She will always know her mother loved her very much and she was trying to change her life for her. While I was Rayne's mentor, she had started back going to school, and she had also written a book about her life. I will be publishing her book and putting it under Eva's name, making sure that she gets all of the proceeds. Before I leave from up here, I want you all to know that me and my family became Rayne and Eva's family at the end of her life. She will forever be remembered in our hearts."

Bailey started to cry while walking back to her seat, and Reem got up to meet her. It wasn't a dry eye in the building. It was way more people then we thought. As I looked around, there still was no Deja. I hope she showed her face before the end of the service.

DEJA

Today was the day Rayne was being laid to rest and I wasn't missing this for the world. I knew I had to be nice to Jace for him even to consider letting me go. We had talked about it and he ignored me like I wasn't talking to him. While he was downstairs I decided to find me something to wear to the funeral. I even asked him to go with me, that way he would know I was coming back home. While I was digging in the closet, I found a little ass gun that I knew had to be Jace's. It was so little it could fit right in my purse. I grabbed it and put it right inside my purse, then laid my clothes out on the bed.

After my clothes were laid out, I went into the bathroom to take care of my hygiene. Once I made it to the bathroom, I turned the shower on to the temperature I liked, then I got in. While I let the water run down my body, thoughts of Rayne not being here came to mind, and the tears started to fall. I knew I had to get the hell out of here before I was next. Knowing that somebody so close to me died at the hands of a man, I could not let this happen to me.

After washing and rinsing a couple of times, I jumped out of the shower and headed back to the room to get myself dressed. I wanted to text Ky and Bailey, but he had been letting me use my phone only to talk to my mom or Tee so that they won't suspect anything. Once I oiled my skin, I slipped my clothes on, then I headed to my vanity to fix my hair and throw some light make-up on my face.

"Where the fuck you think you are going, Deja?"

"Today is Rayne's funeral."

"You ain't going to that shit, so you might as well take that shit off."

"Jace I'm going to this funeral, it's something I can not miss."

"Deja, who the fuck you talking to?" I hurried and got my ass up in case he tried to hit me from behind.

"Come on Jace, why don't you come with me?"

"Deja, I'm not going and neither are you. So take those fucking clothes off now!"

"No, Jace I'm getting the fuck out of this house."

"Yo, since you been back from that center, ya ass been talking mad shit. They must have taught you girl power, because your little ass been acting fucking tough." As soon as those words left his mouth, he punched me right in my face with his closed fist, and I fell back on the bed. I felt my eye close up instantly. I jumped up off the bed then punched his ass right back in the face.

"I wish ya bitch ass stop fucking hitting me, Jace."

He grabbed his lip and when he saw it was bleeding, this nigga went crazy on my ass, hitting me like I was a fucking punching bag. I laid on the floor, curled up in a knot, acting like I was knocked out. Jace just left the room and went downstairs, like he always did. I never understood how he could just beat the shit out of me, then either leave the house or just go downstairs and watch TV. After he left the room, I crawled over to my purse and grabbed the little gun that I put in there earlier, then headed downstairs. I was in all types of pain but I knew I need to get the fuck out of here.

"Yeah man, I'll be there in a little bit let me get a shower. Then I'll meet you on the block," I heard Jace talking to somebody on the phone. I knew I could have waited until he left, but I also knew he wasn't gone let me be unless one of us was dead and it wasn't gone be me. Once I made it into the living room I made sure to stand right in front of him with the gun pointed at him.

"All I ever did was love you. You were my first everything, and you did nothing but hurt me. Why Jace, why couldn't you just love me like I loved you?"

"I do love you baby, now put that gun away. I promise I won't ever hurt you again."

"Jace, you say that shit all the time, but you stay beating the shit out of me. Where I'm going today is a close friend of mine's funeral. Do you wanna know how she died, Jace? Probably not, but Imma tell ya sorry ass anyway. Her baby's father brutally beat her and then put her in a car trunk and left her in a vacant lot. The day you made me get in the car with you; I just knew it was gone be the end of my life. Until I woke up today, I said I ain't gone let that shit happen."

"Come on Ma, you can go ahead to the funeral. Do you still want me to go with you?" Jace asked while walking up to me. As soon as I felt like he was too close I pulled the trigger.

"OUCH FUCK! Deja, you shot me," Jace screamed, falling back on the couch.

"I told you to stay away from me, Jace." I turned to walk over to the coffee table and grabbed Jace's keys to his car.

"You can leave if you want to, but when I find you, Imma kill you. Do you think Imma let you live happily with someone else? That nigga Taji love you, I can tell by all the text messages he been sending you. Once you leave this house, I'm coming to find you, and I'm killing you."

I walked back over to him and pointed the gun at him shot him right through the head. I was scared and I was shaking, but I knew this is what had to happen for me to live my life without being in fear. Once I had my phone, purse, and the keys to Jace's car, I left out the door. I had to hurry up before I missed Rayne's service. I didn't care how I looked, I wouldn't miss it for the world.

* * *

I was still in a state of shock, walking into Willie Watkins Funeral home. Everyone was still in attendance. It was a small ceremony, and I was grateful for that, considering how fucked up I looked. I walked straight up to the front to see Rayne one last time. The funeral home director stopped talking when he saw me walking to the casket.

"I'm so sorry I'm late baby, but I refused to miss seeing you one last time. It almost cost me my life, but I made it. We didn't know each other a long time, but in the little bit of time we did, we started a bond that couldn't be broken. We shared plenty of stories about our rough lives. I'm so mad at you for not listening to me, and leaving the center. I'm not gone fight with you about it right now, but when I get there, we are definitely fighting. Rest in paradise, my baby, and know that as long as I have breath in my body, I'll make sure Eva is straight. I love you Rayne King, until we meet again."

After my speech I turned to leave out of the funeral home, but Taji jumped up and grabbed me before I got to leave. He pulled me in for a hug and the tears started falling down my face.

"I'm so sorry, I didn't mean to hurt your feelings. All the messages that were sent to you were from Jace."

"I know baby, I knew it wasn't you. Come on, let's go get you cleaned up," Taji grabbed my hand and we left out of the funeral home.

Today would be a day. I would never forget I had to take the life of my first everything to see one of my closest friends one last time.

FIVE

TAJI

Seeing Deja all beat the fuck up made me furious. I saw her when she first walked into the funeral home. Her eye was swollen shut, her lip was busted and bloody. Her buttons on her shirt were missing so her shirt was open a little and her hair was all over the place. Not to mention she was walking in slow motion, slouched over like she was in pain. I wanted to jump up and grab her, but when she started her speech, I just let her finish. Then when she went running out of the door, I stopped her. While pulling her in for a hug, I assured her that everything was going to be alright.

"Taji, please get me out of here."

"Do you wanna go to the hospital or the center?"

"I wanna go where it'll just be you and me. I don't want no company, and I don't feel up to talking to anyone."

"Alright, well we can go to Reem and B's house. My room is all the way on the other side of the house. You'll be cool there."

The ride to the crib was quiet as hell. I'm not sure what happened, but Deja seemed off. We were now pulling up to the crib. I had already shot Reem a text letting him know where we were. Once I parked the car, I helped Deja out, then walked her in the house. When we made it in the house, I grabbed her hand and walked her to my room. She sat on the bed just staring at the wall.

"Talk to me baby, tell me what happened?"

"He's dead, Taji."

"Who's dead baby?"

"Jace, I shot him. I shot him," Deja screamed while crying hysterically.

"Alright baby, calm down. Everything will be fine." I assured her while rubbing her back.

"He beat me because I told him I was coming to Rayne's funeral. He didn't want me to see you again. I couldn't miss her funeral Taji, and he wouldn't let me come."

"Shssssss, I know baby, I know. Where is Jace's body at, and where is the gun you used?"

"The gun is in my purse at the funeral home in Jace's car, and he's at his house in the living room."

I hurried and pulled my phone out of my pocket and dialed Reem's number.

"Yo cuz, what's up? we on our way there now."

"Did y'all leave the funeral home yet?"

"Nah. Why what's up?"

"I need one of y'all to drive Jace's car, we need to get rid of that bitch, and we need to get rid of Deja's purse that's in there to.? I'll explain everything when y'all get here, and see if Tee can come sit with her until we go handle some shit."

"Alright, I'll be there in like fifteen minutes."

After we disconnected our phone call, I helped Deja up and carried her into my bathroom.

"Come on Deja, let's get you cleaned up."

"My body is so sore, Taji."

"You might need to be seen by a doctor, baby."

"Not right now, please."

"How about we get one to come to the house so you won't have to leave."

Once we made it to the bathroom, I turned the water on hot as she could stand it, so she could soak her body since she was sore.

"Ok, I'm about to leave out while you take your bath."

"Taji, please don't go. Can you help me out of my clothes, please?"

I wanted to object, but I wasn't gone leave her hanging. I walked over to her and helped her remove her clothes. The bruises that were all over her body angered me.

"I'm so sorry Taji, I really am."

"Baby, you don't have to be sorry."

"I shouldn't have left the center that day. I should have listened to y'all, then I wouldn't be in this situation."

"It's not your fault, and I'm not gone let you blame yourself for this."

After Deja was completely naked and the water was finished, I helped her get in the tub. Then I left out of the bathroom.

"No Taji, don't leave me," Deja yelled right before I left out.

"I need to go handle something. Tee and Samaad just pulled up and she's gone come sit with you until I get back," I assured her while kissing her forehead. As soon as I left out the bathroom Tee was knocking on my room door.

"Where is she?"

"She's soaking in the bathtub. Take care of her until I get back."

"Now you know you don't have to tell me that. I got her always, and they're out front waiting for you," Tee sassed.

I headed outside where the fellas were, so we could get this shit cleaned up.

Before I headed out the front door, Ky and B called me into the living room.

"How is she doing, Taji?"

"Man, she's fucked up. She is gone to need a lot of counseling. I think she killed that nigga. I mean she said she shot him, but I'm about to go see if he's dead."

"Oh my God, my poor baby."

"Oh yeah, can you call one of the doctors to come check her out? She doesn't wanna go out of the house."

"Alright, I'll call one up right now," Ky said. After talking to the girls, I made my way outside.

"Hey cuz, what's the move?"

"Well we need to hit Jace's crib up to see if that nigga is dead. If he ain't, we killing his bitch ass on the spot."

"Wooh, wait a minute, what you mean to see if he died?" Samaad asked.

"Baby girl said she shot him, so if she did and he's dead, we need to clean this shit up and get rid of the gun, car, and his body."

"Damn, man, she probably fucked up," Reem said.

"Yeah, she is really fucked up."

"Well, let's go handle it so that we can get you back here with ya girl," Brodie demanded.

We all piled up in Brodie's truck and headed to Jace's crib. We needed to see if he was dead to know what the next steps were going to be. Brodie turned a half hour drive into a ten-minute drive. We were already pulling up to Jace's crib. My ass almost jumped out while the car was still moving, I was so furious. I ran up the steps and tried the door, and it was unlocked. I walked right in, then headed to the living room. Once I made it there, that nigga was as good as dead. He had a bullet straight through his head, and another in his shoulder. Baby girl gave this nigga a straight headshot, making sure he was never hurting her again.

"Damn, she offed that nigga," Reem said as he entered the living room.

"Yo Samaad, shoot Ray and them a text giving them the address and the code so they'll know what type of call this is," Brodie demanded.

"Go up to the room Taji, and see if Deja has any important papers or anything around here. Imma give them the order to torch this bitch after the get rid of the body."

I did as Reem said, with Samaad following behind me. I felt bad that Deja had to kill him. But if she didn't do it herself, she probably would have hated me for doing it.

EPILOGUE

Deja

So it's been six months and life has been great for me. I'm now a mentor/counselor at the center. When Ky and Bailey came to me with the job offer, I was all for it. I'm living in my own house just having a ball, and enjoying life. Today Bailey and Reem got married and now we all were having it at the reception.

"Look at you fat mama," I teased Tee as she walked to the table.

"Deja, shut up and stop calling me fat."

"Yeah, stop calling my baby fat." Maady said. While walking up behind Tee and grabbing her by her waist.

"Well you are fat, but it's for a good cause. Don't worry, when you are done pushing my godson out, we can hit the gym, and shut up Maady I'll call her what I want."

Yes y'all heard right, Tee and Samaad were expecting their first child in five months. They were doing good and I was happy for Tee. She got her a good man, someone that could tame her mean ass.

"Ladies and gentlemen, please stand and welcome Mr. and Mrs. Price," the DJ announced.

Reem and Bailey came walking in with matching outfits on. I guess they went and changed there clothes so they could get comfortable. They had the biggest wedding and everything was so beautiful. There were so many people in attendance, Taji's dad even came down for the wedding. Speaking of Taji, my baby sang the shit out of those songs for the wedding. His voice was amazing and I was glad his dad was here to see it.

Taji's studio is doing great and next month he will be releasing an album for his girl group, and a solo album for himself. So, yes we making moves over here. Oh, and you noticed I said my baby. We decided to make it official about a month ago. I kept pushing him away, but he wasn't trying to hear that.

"What you over here doing, baby?" Taji asked.

"Nothing, just messing with Tee. Where's Eva at?"

"She's over there playing with the twins."

My little Miss Eva was doing great, and she was all Ky and Brodie needed to make their life complete. The adoption was final and they had no worries. Life was great for everybody at the moment. I still have some issues, but it's nothing my therapist can't help me get through. Plus, I have a whole new family other than Tee, my mom, and her mom. In such a little time, I've gained so much and I am very thankful. It's times I felt like taking my life and hell, at times, I thought I wasn't gone make it out alive. But guess what, I came out still standing.

Domestic Violence is an abuse of human rights within a relationship where there should be love. You may think it's love, but if someone is hitting on you it's not love its abuse. Remember it doesn't always have to end badly, and there's life after abuse...

SUSCRIBE/SUBMIT

Pen Palace Publishing is currently accepting submissions from NEW and experienced authors in Urban Fiction, African American Romance, Street Lit, Women's/Contemporary Fiction...

If you have a finished manuscript that you would like to send for consideration, please send the following to :

ppp.publishing1@gmail.com

1)Contact information

2)Synopsis

3)First 3 chapters in a Word DOC

If Pen Palace has any interest in your work, the full novel will be requested.

Text Shan to 22828 to stay up to date with new releases, sneak peeks, contest, and more...

Or sign up Here

Check your spam if you don't receive an email thanking you for signing up.

CPSIA information can be obtained
at www.ICGtesting.com
Printed in the USA
LVHW05s1417170618
580995LV00009B/471/P

9 781981 851690